Francis Bede lives and writes in Tasmania

Bede, Francis (editor)
Alfonso: his vignettes - 1936 – 1968
ISBN: 978-0-9806289-5-1
Copyright © 2022 Francis Bede
Cover design Francis Bede
First Published Bad Clergy Press November 2022

Alfonso: His Vignettes - 1936 to 1968

– chosen and edited by Francis Bede

By the same author:

Bad Clergy – a question in five fantasies

God in the Human Machine – a theobiography

Houdini Weaned on Fear - poems

Introduction

The minor author, Alfonso Drill, thinker, bon-vivant, well read, and once a man of religion, was known among family and close friends to be somewhat of a literary non conformist. He did not care much for publication; it was as an amusement to himself and a private record of his casting of his jaundiced eye over the world. And when his granddaughter asked why he wrote in this style, as what is presented here, the author's reply to her was a curt "Well someone had to do it!" Upon seeing her looking bewildered, for she was quite young, he softened and told her that he was always looking for new ways to express himself. He was bored with literary conventions. Perhaps he was not good enough to write in the orthodox way. He said that he always liked the letter L. It was the beginning letter for English words which describe many powerful human characteristics: love, loyalty, liberty, left handedness (that the author was!), loony, life, luminary, like and the like. Thus, in his L period of writing, his thoughts and observations fell onto the page in the deckled form of the letter L.

Some years later Francis Bede had made the acquaintance of this the author's granddaughter, her name being Eloise: she being the daughter of Francesca, second daughter to Alfonso and Florence, who was also the step niece to Alfonso's boy, Charlton. After their first encounter in the book department at Myer Melbourne, they agreed to meet again. On their second meeting one moonlit evening on the empty steps of the National Gallery of Victoria Eloise had related her grandfather's writing deeds to him. They met again in his St Kilda flat and in her possession were, what she believed to be, the more eloquent of Alfonso's manuscripts and she wondered whether Francis, an aspiring young writer, would like to take them, fashion them, edit them, collaborate with her on them, and publish them. He might even wish to call them his own. Francis asked why? Her reply was that he was too young to be labelled a cynic like her grandfather had been. It was a harsh stigma she felt she needed to ameliorate. Francis said he might. He was secretly in love with her and he wanted to please her.

Alfonso was certainly prolific. But the various manuscripts Eloise had presented to Francis Bede were somewhat unwieldy to him and after much negotiation, for Eloise was forthright in her opinion of her grandfather's works they agreed that a reasonable selection would suffice. It was a reality that in the late 1970's in a world of sport and other spectacular entertainments, such writings as Alfonso's were sure to bore the froth off even the worst poured beer. Thus, mindful of the power of the ever-expanding Global Amusement Arcade Francis Bede chose, with Eloise's approval, a selection of Alfonso's more polemical and provocative discoursing; those which might resonate enough to generate in those questioning inclined readers a slight nod of approval.

Two Hundred and Twenty-Seven Vignettes

Vignette i

It is impossible

For children to understand

The cruel slaughter

Of creatures

Adults pursue,

And some

Will grow to indifference

And others to horror.

There is condemnation for those who enter into slaughter. For the law of Nature is to set free in life the feeling of respect and dignity. For what Nature does with this law is to strengthen a human desire for harmony. Nature does this through its creatures in order that benevolence might be fulfilled in all who walk the earth not according to their lusts, but according to their love.

Vignette ii

Some corrupt officials believe
That by taking a bath
Adding their blood
Honey and soda water
Their self hatreds
Will dissolve
And also become liquid,
And only then might they pull the plug.

It comes from the fear that they may find themselves not as they wish, that there may be internal quarrelling, jealousy, anger, hostility, gossip, conceit, and disorder. They fear that when they do it again, they may be humbled before the law, and they may have to mourn over what they have not repented for; the impurity, corruption, bribery and pecuniary sensuality they have practiced.

Vignette iii

Upon the spot of death
A pile of sugar lay
And upon the coffin's head
A sugar pile also lay,
For there is nothing worse
Than fond memories
Lost
In this period of grief.

Those who dismiss the tears which flow from sorrowful eyes, who believe in a life thereafter, who decree tears are no reward for the good of this world, should be ignored. Instead, there are the physical memories, and if need be, cuts and tattoos placed on living bodies. Then nothing is scattered, nothing is lost, nor is melancholy waived.

Vignette iv

There was once a tribe of runners
Who ran to keep fit,
And when a disease
Plagued the tribe
The fastest believed
They could outrun it
By running
Even faster.

And since they are surrounded by an expectant gathering of witnesses, let them also lay aside every weight and burden which clings so closely, and let them run with endurance the race which is set before them. And they who run for cleansing shall renew their strength; they shall mount up with wings like eagles; they shall run and not be weary; then afterwards when they walk, they shall not faint.

Vignette V

Disappointed with Democracy
A congregation of citizens
Went back to an old tradition
Of banishing the Devil,
By singing of their sins
And the sins of others
And by banging pot and pans
And throwing sticks and stones at Him.

They left the elementary doctrine of the modern libertarian and went on to paganism; not laying again the foundations for the sufferance of corrupt works and of faith toward politics, and of instruction about promises; nor the laying on of policies, the resurrection of insolvent ideologies, and miscounts at the ballot box.

Vignette vi

An ancient God
Placed mirrors over the earth
Ten metres from the surface
Infusing within the reflections
The phrase 'you are God'
For everyone to see,
And still the people of the world
Chose to look elsewhere.

Faith seems therefore to be the only assurance of things hoped for, the conviction of things not seen. And by it believers receive little direction. By their faith they must believe that the universe was created by the word of a timeless God, so that what is imagined cannot originate out of things visible to them.

Vignette vii

Men who feel aggrieved by women
Draw images of them on paper
And over the images
They write all their troubles
Concerning love and money,
They then give the papers
To a teenage boy
Who burns them on a pyre.

The women are daughters of men, they are men's children. They are confident, walking upright together or alone, seeing all around, their independence shown by their striding, their fashion defining their identities. They will talk when men are likely to listen, they will listen when men are likely to talk.

Vignette viii

For survivors of an exploded bomb
It is a tragedy and a disaster
Beyond their comprehension,
For the perpetrators
The shrapnel
Symbolises in them
The ills of their own lives
And the hatred plaguing them.

Dark waters close in over bombers taking their minds; the deep surround them; weeds are wrapped about their heads. They lay beneath mountains. They go down to their depths where mental stalactites close around them forever; there is no life in their dungeon, and when their lives begin fainting away, they choose destruction.

Vignette ix

Some who are bullied
Feel so powerless
They make their bullies
Into effigies of pop stars,
And with the bully's name on them
They throw the effigies
At screaming teenage girls
Waiting for their idols at airports.

Because they draw upon themselves and mock bullies with their effigies, when their hearts are far from them, and fear of them is a commandment taught by bullies, therefore, behold, they do wonderful things with their imaginations; and the actions of their adversaries shall perish, and bully influence shall be mocked for all time.

Vignette X

A Catholic priest
Asked a sexual therapist
To exorcize his genital organs,
So that his reproductive energies
Could no longer be confused with
The demoniacal spell
First cast over him
Because of his celibacy.

He so wishes that all were as he himself is. But he has his own gift from his God, one of one kind and one of another. To the unmarried and the widowers, he'll tell them that it is good they remain celibate as he is. But if he really cannot stop burning with passion, his therapist tells him he should leave the priesthood and marry one of them.

Vignette xi

Sword dancers were employed

By a stock broking firm

To expel bad luck

By hewing and slashing

Long strips of fly paper thrown in the air,

The strips then minutely cut

And flushed down

The chairman's toilet.

The dancers were under the direction of the accountant who provided the music in the office which included cymbals, harps, and lyres for the service of the dancers. Accounts receivable blew trumpets and accounts payable played flutes so that they build an atmosphere appropriate for the sacred dance.

Vignette xii

One might wonder
When studying the history
Of human killing
Sanctioned or otherwise,
Whether human nature
Is out of control
Or it is through Nature
That humans kill.

But understand that each day presents itself with incidents of difficulty. For such killers will be lovers of adrenalin, lovers of noise, arrogant, abusive, heartless, unappeasable, brutal, not loving peace, reckless, swollen with conceit, lovers of power, lovers of control; while having the appearance of humanity, but denying all its possibilities.

Vignette xiii

There was recently a man
Who walked the Earth
Healing the sick
And preaching love over hatred
Seen by sceptical priests
Who said there can be only one healer,
For he was immortalized
Millenniums before.

This man was a simple sower who came to randomly sow. Some seeds fell along the path, and the birds came and devoured them, spreading them with their dung. Other seeds fell on rocky ground, where they did not have much soil, and amazingly some sprang up, but sadly, when the sun rose, they were scorched.

Vignette xiv

If Christianity is true
Then it can be
Of no real importance;
If it is not true
Then it is
A tragic disaster
From which humanity
Will never recover.

It is said that all Scripture is breathed out by God and is profitable for teaching, for correction, and for training in righteousness, that the man of God may be competent; equipped for every good work. Everything the man of God says is tested and what is good is held fast. The sum of it counted as what is successfully persuaded.

Vignette xv

'We are certainly civilized'
Said a New Yorker recently;
'In ancient times
The end of the year
Was celebrated
In an orgy of unbridled flesh
And now it is celebrated
With unbridled wealth.'

Today or tomorrow, people will go into such and such a town and spend a year there and trade and make a profit. Celebrations the mist which appears for a little time and then vanishes. What has been is what will be, and what has been done is what will be done, and there is nothing new under the sun.

Vignette xvi

If the scriptures
Are to be believed
They are left
To the believers;
If the scriptures
Are to be analysed
They are left
To the scholars.

Atheists hope the analysed scriptures will come to them soon, and scholars are writing about them without delay, so that invited atheists may know how to behave in the households of God believers, which are the churches of the imagined God, appointed pillars and upholders of religious truth, which, in the name of dissent, atheists need not see.

Vignette xvii

Oh were it that true history

Could be like flawless diamonds;

Instead there is just

Broken rubble from

Endless volcanoes

For short

And mortal lives

To sift through.

Nothing should be covered up which can be revealed, or hidden which can be known. Whatever is created in the dark should be shown in the light, and what is whispered in behind closed doors should be proclaimed in public. And no participant is hidden from sight, but all are naked and exposed to the eyes of whoever needs to see.

Vignette xviii

And when the world was dark
The wise said all must make candles
In the image of God;
And while none
Could make such an image
The world lay in darkness
Until a maverick made
A candle in the human image.

And then came the Word, and the Word was through the candle, and the Word was human. Humanity was in the beginning living with imagery. All imaginary things were made through it, and without imagination there was not anything to be made. In the imagination was life, and life became the light of humanity.

Vignette xix

In ancient culture

It was taboo

For the Divine

To touch the ground

With their feet;

And yet today

No such taboo applies

To entertainment superstars.

The Entertainment Divine hide their feet at love feasts, and they feast on fame without fear, the Divine being fed by their worshippers; they are as water fills clouds, swept along by winds; as fruitful trees in late autumn, twice alive, harvested; as wild waves of the sea, casting up the foam of their own glory; as wandering stars, for whom the light of the world has been reserved forever.

Vignette xx

It became known
That a serial killer
Wore an eyeless mask;
The same mask
Put on by an ordinary man
Whenever he was about
To watch a killing
On the television.

And there were those about to die who beheld a masked
rider on a pale horse. And its rider's name was Death, and
violent Hades always followed Death around. And Death
gave itself authority over every corner of the Earth, to kill
with gun and bomb, and with starvation and with chemicals
and by the iron hooves of the horse he rode.

Vignette xxi

People wear
Wide brimmed hats
To keep the Sun off them
For they are in the know
Who think like the Mikado,
Firmly believing the Sun
Is not worthy
To shine upon them.

It is better to ascribe to the Sun, ascribe to the Sun's glory
and strength. Ascribe to the Sun the glory due its name;
honour the Sun in the splendour of its brilliance. When the
rays of the Sun warm the waters the rays of the Sun are life
giving; the rays of the Sun are full of majesty.

Vignette xxii

It was thought
The Pope should have an heir
Who must live
Seventeen years
With the poor,
Then he will understand
The true value of life
And the meaning of death.

Instead, the Pope thinks of himself more highly than he ought to think, thinking without sober judgment, without the measure of faith that his God has assigned to him. Having gifts that differ according to the grace given to him, he does not use them. And likewise, having given up natural relations with women he is consumed with passion for Mary, imagining unmentionable acts with her.

Vignette xxiii

Fanatical sports fans

Hide in darkness

Before they make the pilgrimage

To their sacred home ground,

And for four whole days

They abstain from alcohol and sex

That they may have an influence

On their team's performance.

And seeing the crowd, they go up into the stands, and when they sit down, the atmosphere overwhelms them. And they open their mouths and chant 'Blessed are our team in spirit, for ours is the home ground of Success. Blessed are those who support our team, for they shall be comforted and they shall inherit much fan Bonding.'

Vignette xxiv

Legend has it
That it is the Sun
Which the foetus dreams of,
For when a child
First screams
It is out of fear
Of the bright light
Which meets its eyes.

The child will then search for it and get to know it. It will know why it rises and why it sets. And when it rises the child will discern its actions from afar. It will search out the Sun's path and be acquainted with all its ways. Even before a word is on the child's tongue, behold, it will know much of it.

Vignette xxv

There are many people
The world over
Who grey prematurely,
And it has long been thought
That it is because
They have seen
Something while a child
They shouldn't have.

Inasmuch as many have undertaken to write of things which have traumatized them, just as those who were also eyewitnesses, it seems therapeutic to do so, having carried such things closely for a long time past; and to write an orderly account means that they have a record of certain things which they did not understand.

Vignette xxvi

The famous who talk of
Their intimate details
Make of it such a spectacle
That eventually
It will not be enough
For consumers to believe
What they say,
They will want the evidence.

Those who live according to attention seeking set their minds on things associated with attention, but those who live according to integrity, set their minds on things concerning integrity. To those who set their minds on attention seeking is brought contempt, but setting the mind on integrity brings life and peace. Those who are in realm of attention seeking can never please themselves.

Vignette xxvii

New science

Having drawn inspiration from old theories

Shows its reverence

By disproving them;

Established religion

Having drawn inspiration from old theologies

Shows its reverence

By dismissing them.

Two people together went into church to pray, one a preacher and the other a scientist. The preacher, standing alone, prayed thus: 'God, I thank you that I am not like others; atheists, heathens, adulterers, or even like this smelly scientist. I fast twice a week; I give glimpses of all that I absorb.' And the scientist, standing alone, simply said, 'God, be merciful to me, a questioner!'

Vignette xxviii

If it is too difficult

For a sceptic

To disprove something

The sceptic is told to believe,

Therefore the truth

Presented to the believer

Is no different

To a sceptic's truth.

If anyone teaches a different doctrine and disagrees with the words of someone like Jesus Christ, he is accused of being puffed up with conceit. He is accused of having a craving for controversy and he quarrels over the meaning of words. The sceptic is accused of creating dissension, and friction causing depravity of mind and depravity of truth; who simply sees righteous godliness as merely a means for aggression.

Vignette xxix

An ideology had grown

That black is actually white,

And the ideology

Became folklore

And a superstition

And a ritual

Which became a festival

Establishing the ideology's truth.

The tongue is a small organ, yet it can boast of doubtful things. And the tongue is a fire which can bring in a world of lies, misunderstandings and confusion. The boasting tongue is set prominent over the body, dribble staining the whole of it, setting on fire the entire course of a life, and with it the fires of tragedy and woe.

Vignette xxx

May the Christmas tree stand

May all good-will venture in

May joy be invigorating

May the children get presents

May the roast lamb be moist

May the drinks keep flowing,

And on this stand-out day of the year

What else should matter?

The Christ in the manger is heir to earthly misery. And while he is like a child, and although he is the owner of everything sad, he remains under the guardianship of preachers and prophets until the date of his return, set by his heavenly father. And moreover, only he is for preachers to speak of.

Vignette xxxi

Whichever is the real soul?

An abstraction

Which only Heaven

Has the key

Or the mind

When its living bearer

Is preparing the best of it

For death and beyond.

When a believer's earthly home is destroyed, there is a place offered by the believer's God which is ready, a dwelling not made with human hands, and eternal in the heavens. While in this earthly home the believer groans; who longs to feel eternally safe in Heaven. And yet there are many who pray their soul won't be put there naked.

Vignette xxxii

She felt his stomach cancer
By ingesting meat
Rancid and maggot filled
And passing the remains
Through her digestive tracts,
So that her brother
Dying in the next room
Might yet be saved.

By this she gives love, which in desperation, she is laying down as pain for her brother. And if cynics see her and her brother in need, but close their hearts against them, how can empathy abide in them? Let them not criticise in talk but discover their own love through remorse. Her deed might be of no avail but it doesn't matter.

Vignette xxxiii

It is believed among certain God worshippers
They will not reach heaven
Unless all waste displaced from their bodies
Is put in a safe place
And buried after death along with the carcass;
The sacraments which release their spirit
They believe will also vaporize
Their bodily germs.

They enjoyed their bodily functions, and they dutifully watched their workings. They knew they had good processions and abiding ones. Therefore, they kept their earthly confidence, which had great rewards. For they need to endure bodily, so that by doing the will of God they will receive what is promised.

Vignette xxxiv

A fair maiden asked

The young soldiers marching by

'Where is your death?'

'It is in Flanders Field yonder

Fair maiden

And should we survive

And pass this way again

Our death will be in remembering your beauty.'

She is their lovely idol; they shall not want. She'll have them lie down in green pastures in peace. She leads them beside still waters. She restores their feelings. Even though they walk through valleys of the shadow of death, they will fear no evil, for she is with them.

Vignette xxxv

It is speculated
That human life
Is bound with that
Of the lives of animals
And of fish,
By those who have
Webbing between
Their toes.

At twenty-nine pious Aria was diseased in her feet, and her disease became severe. She did not seek a priest but sought help from a doctor. And disabled Aria continued to live with her husband, and care for her children, and she died aged seventy-four. She was cremated, and was warmly memorialised by her family.

Vignette xxxvi

The bond between
A woman and her dog
Was such that
She transfused
Their bloods,
Then one will become
The other
Should either prematurely die.

Now concerning her pet dog. She is aware that she knows it well. This knowledge might puff her up, but love builds her up. If she only imagines that she knows something, she might not yet know as she ought to know. And when she shows her love for her dog, it will instinctively know. Therefore, as to the preparation of food for her dog, it always knows it is the one.

Vignette xxxvii

Wouldn't it be nice

If every human believed

That their lives were bound

With an animal's life

But not knowing how;

Hunters would hesitate

Speedsters would slow down

And the cruel remain still.

Human fear and dread shall be attached to every animal of the Earth and to every bird of the Skies, to everything which creeps on the ground and all the fish of the sea. Into humans humility can be received. Every moving thing which lives shall provide wise thought for them.

Vignette xxxviii

Her brother is an eagle

His sister is an owl

His life is an eagle's

Her life is an owl's,

The eagle has a human sister

The owl has a human brother

The eagle lives like a brother

The owl lives like a sister.

Respect is patient and kind; respect does not envy or boast; it is not arrogant or rude. It does not insist on its own way; it is not irritable or resentful; it does not rejoice at wrongdoing, but rejoices when truth is found. Respect bears all things, imagines all things, hopes all things, endures all things.

Vignette xxxix

A cricket ball

Is handed around spectators

Who shout all their troubles

At it,

Then the ball is passed back to the fast bowler

Who bowls a half volley

For the batsman

To hit out of the ground.

But first the cricket ball, on which the lot of all misery fell, is presented to the chief umpire who holds it high, a symbol of atonement, to the troubled mass of spectators, before it is then batted away as the scapegoat, way away into the suburban wilderness.

Vignette xl

There is a way the Jesus Christ

May still be living on Earth as God

For humanity has his mind as a totem

Which it has kept

Since Jesus' death,

And all who have his mind

Feel that God

Is within them.

And they make for themselves carved images of his mind, in a likeness of Heaven above, and a likeness of the Earth surrounding them, and that which lies in its bowels. They set their carved images in children's playgrounds and bow down to them before burning them, for fear that Jesus may, in his human weakness, be jealous.

Vignette xli

It may be taken as a prophetic sign

When cannons are fired

To celebrate religious authority

In the vicinity of a bird flock,

The noise causing

A raining down

Of bird droppings

Upon the heads of the crowd.

And for every nation of humankind to live peacefully on the face of the Earth, having determined allotted cultures and boundaries for their dwelling places, they should then seek for themselves a personal God, so that they might feel their way towards such a God. And where birds fly, so should they also follow them.

Vignette xlii

The first casualty
Of social change
Is a country's history,
And what is left to remember it
Are but the celebrations
Of the newest social order
Which relies on mythology
To date the history's relevance.

One person might esteem a celebration day as better than another, while another might esteem all such days as alike. Each one fully convinced in one's own mind. But when a National Day is observed, it is in honour of country. The dancing and eating is in honour of country, and thanks is given to country. The ones who abstain, abstain despite their alienation.

Vignette xliii

A native clothed in traditional dress

Walks toward a mechanical door

Which opens

As if by magic,

The same native now clothed

In a business suit

Walks towards many doors

Which do not open automatically.

And respectful now is this man who seeks not the counsel of magicians, nor stands in the way of mechanical progress, nor sits in the seat of the impatient; he instead delights in the fair entry and on this he meditates. He is like a tree on the bank of a river which yields its fruit in its season, and which does not wither.

Vignette xliv

There was a culture when premature death
Was common for the healthy
When the spirit
Was as healthy as the body alive,
And no vigour was then lost
In the ethereal world
Of Heaven and Earth
Which live in harmony together.

And the living felt sure of good things, things which belonged to energy. And the deceased's work wasn't overlooked, nor their love in working alongside the living. And it was the culture's desire that every living individual show similar earnestness in order that they have the full assurance of joy until the end.

Vignette xlv

The man who is first to bulldoze trees

For a new subdivision

Usually gets a sore neck,

And to avoid the pain

Other dozer-men fill their pockets

With sawdust

As a warning

To the angry tree spirits.

For though the dozer-men work within the rules of safety, they are nevertheless confronted with dissent; their fear demonstrated by the whites of their knuckles. For the weapons of tree spirits include divine powers to hinder development. The spirits try to hinder all methods of land clearing, and every lofty opinion concerning the spread of suburbia into their forests.

Vignette xlvi

In a strange metropolis,
The last person to get off
The last train
At the last station
Farthest east from the GPO
Took for herself a sunflower
From a garden nearby
And wore it all day next.

On that same day she went out of her house and went for a long walk to a nearby beach. And great crowds gathered about her, so that eventually she went to the end of a long wharf. And the whole crowd stood together before her. And in parables she told them many things about the sunflower.

Vignette xlvii

It is in night's darkness

When murderers

Reveal to themselves

Their vacant hearts,

And the healer of darkness

Can merely try

To restore justice

Through the power of remorse.

Those who choose to kill have fallen into temptation, into a snare, into many senseless and harmful desires that plunge them into ruin and destruction. For the love of destruction is a root of further kinds of evil. It is through this craving that they have wandered away from any human connection having pierced themselves with many emotional pangs.

Vignette xlviii

In the belief

That no imperfections return

A plastic surgeon

Empties the extracted fat

Into beautiful dolls,

And stands the dolls

On pedestals

For the clients to see.

And so it was that household dolls had come from vanity, and their owners saw in them the manufacturer's lies; the dolls told of false dreams and gave empty consolation. Thus, disillusioned doll owning people wandered like sheep; they were afflicted for lack of a true maker, but thinking they were fools they became wise instead.

Vignette xlix

Electroconvulsive Therapy
That succeeds in evicting
Dark moods from the mind,
Does so by the chancy notion
That the brain fluid
Is like a flood coursed river
Which flows similarly
Afterwards as before.

Under these clinical conditions the task is not so much to mitigate depression, nor to win the battle of the moods, nor bring knowledge to the facilitators, nor meaning to the patient, nor favour those with understanding, but allow medicine to attempt its work.

Vignette L

The one found guilty of murder
Laid the blame on the gun
Which he bought from a gun dealer,
Who blames the gun maker
Who blames the legislation
Which blames the right to bear arms
Which blames evil
As the cause of all wrongs.

And if a gun club witness sees a threatening gunman coming and does not sound the alarm, so that the people are not warned, and the gunman starts shooting, and the dead are taken away in tragedy; by the deceased's blood the relatives will inquire into the witness's hand in it.

Vignette li

The gorging of animal flesh

In the home or in restaurants

Means that during these events

The animal is

Life giving and sacred,

And the pen in which it wallowed

Is an illusion

Of uncleanness.

Animal flesh eaters close their minds like rebellious people do, and walk in a flashy way, following their own prejudices; these are eaters who sacrifice at barbeques and make offerings on hot bricks; who sit in public houses, and spend nights in secret places eating animal flesh; the scion of sacred meat coursing in their veins.

Vignette lii

They've hopped into too many beds
These men and women,
And what they know of
Themselves during intimacy
Scares them
And what they know of
The thrill of the new
Scares them also.

But judge them not, lest that one be judged. One must try
not to see the speck in another's eye, when there is a huge
rock in one's own. To avoid being a hypocrite, one first
takes the rock out of one's own eye, and then one will see
clearly enough to take the speck out of another's eye.

Vignette liii

Members of an investment clan
Believe
That if they touch it
Before it reaches maturity,
Their hair will turn white
Their skin will break out in boils
Their eyes will be inflamed
Their tongues gone woolly.

If they cast paper money upon flowing waters, finding it after many days, and given that there might be individual notes left, or a lump, they cannot know whether a disaster has ensued or not. If clouds are full of rain, they may empty themselves upon dirt or out at sea, and if a tree falls south or north, where the tree falls, there it lies.

Vignette liv

A minority surfer sect
Whose hair is blond
And who live on the coastal fringes
Shave their heads in the Spring
When the Roaring Forties blow,
Believing their scattered locks
Will be collected by Eagles
And other birds of prey.

Eagles give power to the faint hearted, and to weaklings hoping that eagles will increase their strength. Even blond youths who faint and are weary, young men who fall exhausted, are they who also wait for the Eagles to renew their strength. They who are satisfied with life are like the youth who are renewed by Eagles.

Vignette lv

As armistice closes in
The bakers of each army
Bake loaves in the guise of the enemy
To be eaten when armistice concludes,
For these armies have had enough
And do not wish to return
To their families
Hungry and defeated.

The souls of all soldiers who have died have not sinned. The sons shall not suffer for the iniquity of their parents, nor shall the parents suffer for the iniquity of their sons. The righteousness of the righteous shall be upon one's conscience, and the wickedness of the wicked shall be upon one's conscience.

Vignette lvi

So that they keepsake their souls
The exclusive people talk together
After celebrating the last supper
In an exclusive language
That is hidden,
For they are guaranteed
The attention of their saviour
By the way they speak.

Likewise, a spirit helps them in their conversations. For they might not understand each other as they ought, but the spirit itself intercedes for them with a groaning too deep for words. And they search their hearts to know what is in the mind of the spirit, because the spirit intercedes for them according to the will of their saviour.

Vignette lvii

They saw each other from a distance

And their eyes

Told of an intense need

That appeared mutual,

And after a few drinks

To bed they went

Despite low self esteem

And their anxieties pending.

Not that they ever spoke of being in need, for they have learned in whatever situation to strive to be content. They know how to be brought from low to high, and they know how to be strong. In any and every circumstance, they have learned the secret of knowing restraint and desire, of living with abundance and with famine.

Vignette lviii

Casanova flirted and flattered
And the women were his
Day and night
One after another,
And which of them
Gave sex for love?
And which of them
Gave love for sex?

Casanova gave to the women their conjugal rights, and likewise the women to Casanova. For the women did not have authority over their own bodies, but Casanova had. Likewise, Casanova did not have authority over his body, but the women had. They couldn't deprive each another, except by agreement for a limited time, so that they may devote themselves to rest and perhaps reunite again.

Vignette lix

Corporations also make sacrifices

To gods

And some are macabre

Like hanging a janitor

Like drawing and quartering a clerk

Like beheading a tea lady,

To appease the gods of shareholders

When profits have decreased.

A junior clerk was taken to a place called The Skull, and there he was crucified. And the staff cast lots over his desk belongings. And while they stand by watching him die, the chief clerk scoffs at him, pointing, "His job was to transfer funds to the correct customer accounts. Let him transfer one for himself. If you are truly a Bank Clerk, then save yourself!"

Vignette lx

Some addicts crave so much
They eat themselves alive,
But there are survivors
With a craver's taste
Which is a mixture
Of memories of love
From loved ones
And of love for themselves.

And so, it is that many have undertaken to compile a story of their lives, since, as they were eyewitnesses to a time which they remembered was good, and having followed up on relevant things with family and friends, they aim to write a happier account of themselves.

Vignette lxi

Beware advanced religions
That denies the rituals
Originated in ancient magic,
For in dismissing
Ancient magic as inferior
The seeds of their superiority
Are sown with arrogance
And stained with ignorance.

Still believers will stand fast in their enchantments and mysteries. Perhaps they may be able to succeed; perhaps they may inspire revelation. They are certainly wearied of their many counsels. Let them stand wearily forth and seek salvation, these who search for Heaven, who gaze at the stars, who, at every new moon try hard to make known what is to become of them.

Vignette lxii

A God consecrated bakery
Has created a cupcake
For those believers who still wish
To receive the body of the Christ
But not from the hands of a priest,
And it is called 'teoqualo'
Or god is eaten
And can be purchased any time.

These believers hope the cupcake will help them suppress whatever malice, deceit, hypocrisy and envy they fear they have. Like newborn infants, who long for mother's milk, they may feel nurtured if they have tasted that this God is good. And as they come to this God, a living cake tasty and precious, might they also become as living cupcakes.

Vignette lxiii

Witch doctors roll bones on dirt

And give solace to the ill

Healing for the afflicted

And courage for the fearful,

Priests say devotional prayers

And give solace to the ill

Healing for the afflicted

And courage for the fearful.

Either way, though the chronically ill's outer selves are wasting away, their inner selves are being renewed at the hour. Coping with these afflictions prepares for them an eternal glory beyond all comparison, as they look not to the things that are seen but to the things that are imagined.

Vignette lxiv

In order to make more money
From its devout followers
The Church bought a chocolate factory
For the purpose of mass producing
The image of the Christ on the Cross
As an after-dinner mint,
Even catching out
The lapsed.

When the dinner mint eaters were children, they spoke like children, thought and reasoned like children. After these children grew up and became dinner mint loving adults, they couldn't give up their childish ways. They'd look at themselves in a mirror while eating a dinner mint and saw no adult. In time however, they will know themselves fully, as the playful children they once were.

Vignette lxv

The Vatican,

Standing alone

Like a barren island

In the midst of a vast ocean

Hangs effigies of its inhabitants

Along its impenetrable walls

Hoping the ghosts of its victims

Will bear them away.

The Vatican crew stand arrayed in purple and scarlet, and adorned with gold and jewels and pearls, holding in their hands golden cups full of abominations and the impurities of their perverse morality. And no wonder, for Satan himself stands among them, disguised as the Vatican's angel of light.

Vignette lxvi

They are the future
Those who slaughter body builders
In a core rite of youth
At the Temple of Vitality,
For these shamans believe
After eating the flesh
They will be guarded
Against the enfeeblement of old age.

They hope to inspire other men to better resist the tides of old age, and become more dignified, be strong in their faith, in wisdom, and in steadfastness. Older women likewise might also be reverent in behaviour, caring, wise, upstanding, and not be slavish to material things. All could teach the young what is good and what is important.

Vignette lxvii

There are certain consumers
Who would eat labels and tags
Rather than throw them away,
For they believe that in them
Are the moral and intellectual virtues
Denied to them
By their over valuing
And by their bank balance.

Now, spending is the affirmation of consumption, and the conviction of satisfactions soon to be felt. For by spending, experienced consumers give their recommendation. By faith in the product, they understand that the consumer universe was created in the advertiser's words and images, so that what is seen was not made out of things philosophical.

Vignette lxviii

Humans do not eat Sloth

For good reason,

It is an endangered species

And it is slow

And deliberate

Its movements

Representing patience

And perseverance.

Yet better is the end of a thing than its beginning, and patience in spirit is better than pride in spirit. It is also better that the spirit not become angry, for anger is lodged in the bosom of the disturbed. And let steadfastness have its full effect so that one may feel better for it, and not feel lacking in otherwise false needs.

Vignette lxix

Fencers might eat Rattle Snake

Roller derbiers Echidna

Sumo wrestlers Gorilla

Rock climbers Mountain Goat

Para gliders Condor

Base jumpers Flying Fox

Scuba divers Seal,

If they could.

But then it is quite possible, in the case of these competitors, if bitten by the exotic, having then tasted their apparently heavenly gifts, and having shared in the excitement, that they then fall away to their own detriment, and end up wracked with guilt and self-loathing.

Vignette lxx

Lateral thinking mothers
Slip into their children's porridge
Honey flavoured crow's droppings,
For when the children
Are to have their vegetables
Their plates
Are to be left clean
Like stripped highway carrion.

One mother Abigail, took two loaves and a bag of carrots and five biscuits already prepared, and five bags of peas and a six Brussels sprouts and two bags of spinach, and laid them on the kitchen table. To her children she then said that everything that she prepares shall be food for them. But first she had given them porridge, knowing she can give them anything.

Vignette lxxi

There is a venerated woman
Who lives by a stream
Listening to its murmurs and cries
Understanding what she hears
Before she stands among men
Who've fought from disagreements
Calling them to rationality;
To give ground instead of causing blood.

To this stream there once came a man called Logan, a labourer who gave generously to charity, and who regularly prayed to his God. At about dusk he saw a vision of her, and she said "Logan." And in terror he said, "What is it maiden?" And then she said, "Send me your men friends so I can heal them."

Vignette lxxii

In the chronicles of a man
Renowned for saving the world
A great period of his life
Was never recorded,
And what does it matter
That he may have drank and fornicated
Repented and was born again
Urging others to do the same!

If he was indeed wicked and he then turned away from all his sins and did what was just and right, he shall surely walk down the pathways of the memory of those impressed by him; he shall not die. None of his transgressions shall be remembered against him; only for the righteousness that he has done shall he live.

Vignette lxxiii

Happy are they

Who'd rather someone else

Question their religious belief,

For their happiness depends upon

The hope that

What they hold onto

Will be powerful enough

To get them to Heaven.

Thus, on a mountain they hope to see their God make a feast of food; a feast of well-aged wine, of rich meat full of marrow, of vegetables well cooked. And he will swallow up the shroud of doubt which is ever cast over his believers. They hope he will swallow up death forever; and that their Lord God will wipe away the tears from every face.

Vignette lxxiv

Belief cannot be undressed
And stood naked
Before a piercing sun,
For it will blister
And much wrinkle
That neither night's cool breezes
Nor refreshing rains
Will ever restore.

In the beginning was the Word clothed, and the Word was with clothes, and the Word was made from clothing. And the beneath the Word's clothing was underwear. All things private were clothed by underwear, and without underwear privacy was naked. In clothing there is modesty, and in modesty is the light of concealment. But if this light shines on nudity, nudity cannot become it.

Vignette lxxv

An atheist accuser

Who cast aspersions

On the belief of others

Set up a long mirror

In a town square

And standing before it

Threw stones at it,

Catching glass in his hair.

Then he began to speak boldly in the town square, but when Billy and Graham heard him, they took him aside and explained to him the way of God more accurately. And then they went to a nearby church together, where they declared to the atheist all that God had done for the likes of him, and how God is keeping open the door to faith.

Vignette lxxvi

It comes as no surprise to find

That career leaders

Promoted to provide good example

And caught cavorting with the system

React in a patronizing

And arrogant manner,

For they are as ill

As the powerless cynic.

And there are few people left who are able to empathise with human weaknesses, who, in every respect, though prone to corruption, can still maintain their integrity. Let them with great confidence draw near to people struggling with honesty, that they may exercise truth and ethics, and find in them the trust to help others in times of need.

Vignette lxxvii

Of course politicians will say

That in a democracy

It is every citizen's right

To criticize their policies,

Because they know

That democracy

Guarantees that after an election

There will be more of the same.

Is any among them who are not so sick? Let them who
aren't call on their electorates, and let them talk honestly
with the voters, offering them their humility in the name of
democracy. And the talk of trust will save those politicians
who are still healthy, and the enlightenment will inspire
them.

Vignette lxxviii

Once upon a time

There was a big word bandied about

Called accountability,

But at the time

Those who had power

Thought the word clumsy

And so they decided to replace it

With the word disability.

The empowered who prophesied this change, carefully searched and inquired within themselves, what spirit of confusion would indicate the sufferings of the disempowered and their subsequent miseries. It was revealed to them that the powerful were not only serving themselves but also the future, and that change will be announced through the newspapers who tell nothing but bad news.

Vignette lxxix

It is best not to eat
The Flesh of the Christ
Nor to drink
The Blood of the Christ
In a frenzy,
Because of the fear
That doing either
May stimulate insanity.

Forsaking the right way, these frenzied cannibals have gone astray. They have followed the way of dementia praecox whereby the rational is displaced with the madness for the Christ. And these transgressions may only be rebuked when believers imagine a personal donkey calling on them to redirect their madness elsewhere.

Vignette lxxx

Be it animals

Plants

Or humans

It is meaningful for the tribal

To consume them for the purposes

Of gaining nutrition,

Courage

And divinity.

Every moving thing that lives is food for them, including insects. And for their lifeblood their gods will require a reckoning: from every animal they will require it and from themselves. From them their gods will require a reckoning for the life of any human. Whoever sheds the blood of a human, by humanity shall their blood be shed, for they have made their gods in their own image.

Vignette lxxxi

It is acceptable for some
To bring others
Down to the level
Of their being,
But it is unacceptable
For exceptional others
To raise to a higher level
Anyone.

And as for ones who are simple, they are welcome for their ability to not quarrel over opinions. The smart ones who talk despise the ones who abstain, and then the ones who abstain pass judgment on the ones who talk, contempt having welcomed them all. Who can they be who pass judgment on others? It is before themselves that they stand or fall.

Vignette lxxxii

A way to treat
Humanity's sadness
Is to find the river Styx,
And every day
Cast into it
The daily headlines
Borne by the newspapers
Of the world.

They are the beloved, those who expect a deadening melancholia to test them, as though things metaphysical and out of this world are happening to them. In spite of this they recover insofar as they share with each other their sufferings, from which they may also revive and feel livelier, when a further understanding of it has been revealed.

Vignette lxxxiii

The wise will say
That young ones
Act before they think
While older ones
Think before they act,
And in between
Are the actors
Unsure of what to think.

And, whatever is true, whatever is honourable, whatever is just, whatever is pure, whatever is lovely, whatever is commendable, whatever is sincere, whatever is ethical; if there is any excellence, if there is anything worthy of praise, someone somewhere is thinking about these things.

Vignette lxxxiv

The hunter

Stands over a tiger carcass,

And by the logic

Of his bravery

He will examine his venture

And pay homage to the tiger

As a beast

Greater than himself.

Whoever loves animals loves knowledge, but hunters who hate being disapproved of are stupid. A good person favours all living things, but a person of ego favours only the blood-lusting self. No one enters the world by wickedness, and thus the roots of animal loving will never go. An excellent person is the crown of humanity, but any who brings it shame is like rot and mould.

Vignette lxxxv

There are a very few
Who suffer from
The condition of Gigantism
And they are alone,
But in myth
There were many
And that they even challenged
The mighty Hercules.

A water sprite raised her eyes and saw a weeping giant standing on the bank of a river. It had two horns, and both horns were high, but one was higher than the other, the higher one reaching the clouds. She saw the giant charge upwards and downwards and sideways. Not even Hercules would be able to stand up to it, and there is no one who could be rescued from its power.

Vignette lxxxvi

Political authority
Dismisses criticism of it
With violent words,
And the critics
Have no choice
But to arm their words
And end that authority
With further violence.

If anyone aspires to be a political authoritarian, it is a risky task. A political authoritarian must be above reproach, open-minded, self-controlled, respectable, self loving not self loathing, not duplicitous, not a hypocrite, not quarrelsome, not a lover of power. They must manage their own affairs well, with the dignity of a humble person.

Vignette lxxxvii

In bygone days
So as to not haunt the butcher
A sheep
Was killed as it grazed,
And the killing became inhumane
When the butcher
No longer
Believed in ghosts.

What farmer, having a hundred sheep at his disposal, when one escapes, would not leave the ninety-nine in a holding pen, and go after the escaped one until he finds it? And when he has found it, he lays it on his shoulders, rejoicing. And when he comes home, he calls together his family saying 'Rejoice with me, for I have found the sheep that escaped.'

Vignette lxxxviii

And the company Chairman

Upon the Prospectus entering him

Became violently disturbed,

And in a most astonishing frenzy

He convulsed and distorted his features

Rolling about on the boardroom floor

Shrilly shouting and screaming

Banging his head on the boardroom table.

The board members bound him with chains and rope, but he wrenched the chains apart, and he tore the rope in pieces. No one had the strength to subdue him and they left the room. For hours on end he cried out, rolled about, and stabbed himself with pens. It had not been a very good year.

Vignette lxxxix

It is ironic

In bush life,

That fire starters

Wish that their troubles

Be carried away

By the embers

Which are caught

By the hot winds.

Therefore, as the tongue of fire devours the stubble, and as dry grass sinks down in the flames, so their fire bug roots be as rottenness, and their immoral urges go up like dust; for they have rejected the laws of empathy and compassion, despising the words of all who care for the living world.

Vignette xc

Eaters of processed foods
Who suffer from indigestion
Wear a belt
Of disposables nappies
Around their waists,
In the belief
The evil will be dispensed
When the belt gets heavy.

They are enticed by the sensations of their gullets and they ignore their health. They promise themselves freedom, but they themselves are slaves to convenience. For whatever overcomes such people, to that they are enslaved. Woe to those who lie on beds of convenience or stretch themselves out on couches and eat in this way.

Vignette xci

A man claims he gave up smoking

When, after carrying

The last cigarette butts

Around in his pockets

He cast them into a puddle

And danced a smoker's jig

Shattering his addiction

And easing his heart.

For he lived according to his needs, setting his mind on things he needed, and also according to strong cigarettes setting his mind on their brands. Smoke went out from his nostrils, and a devouring breath issued from his mouth; glowing embers flamed in his lungs. And though he came to know the right thing to do, he had often failed to do it.

Vignette xcii

A divine menu for the secular

may consist of,

Consomme a la Bernhardt

For this is her blood

Filet a l' Americaine

For this is his body

Eclairs au chocolat

For these are their sweets.

May grace and peace be multiplied to those in the secular know. What things that pertain to life and existence, through the knowledge of life, calls them to a living within the limitations which are granted them as precious and promising, so that through them they may be active partakers of the natural, having escaped from the corruption that is superstitious belief.

Vignette xciii

Strangers seen standing near
The Dept. of Treasury
Are thought by some
To be the spirits of budgets
Which have escaped
From adding machines,
And they are less mysterious
In caps and casual wear.

They know well the economic conditions, giving attention to statistics and economic data, for wealth does not last forever. When money is scarce, they wait for economic growth to appear and for investment to go into innovation. Then manufacturers will provide people with new clothing, and employees a raise. There will be enough money for food, and maintenance of homes.

Vignette xciv

There is a flower pot
Standing in the middle
Of an insurance company's forecourt,
In it are flecks of scaly skin
Shod by an executive
Who suffers from psoriasis
Hoping someone sniffs the flower
And bears the disease away.

If not, he shall then be brought to a priest, and the priest shall go into the wilderness, and he will have a look around. Then, if the case of psoriasis can be healed, the priest shall command his assistants to take to the unclean executive two live clean birds and cedar-wood and scarlet yarn and hyssop.

Vignette xcv

There died an ordinary man
Who believed he would
Take with him
The evils of the world,
And then he came back
And found to his horror
Flying machines and lavatories
And that nothing had changed.

For he so loved his world that he gave himself to it. And whoever believed in him thereafter should not perish the way he did, but lead a happy life. For this man did not enter his world to condemn it, but rather he entered his world so that it might get a little better.

Vignette xcvi

Certain young entrepreneurs
Fearing disease might deny them
Have bull ants bite their flesh
From head to toe,
In the belief
That their resident Demons
Plotting their demise
Will be driven away.

Success is their shepherd; they shall not want. It maintains their self belief. It leads them in the direction of contacts for entrepreneurship's sake. Even though they might walk a risky line they fear no competitors. They prepare strategies in order to remain visible in the market place. Their pastures will always be greener. Their vision strong. Their appetites insatiable.

Vignette xcvii

There was once a family,
When the patriarch died
Will never mention his name
For he was kingly and sovereign
Whose rule was so dominant
That out of a strange reverence
The family would only speak of him
As 'The Perfect Tyrant'.

He had said to them "My ego is sufficient for you. My power is perfected from weakness. I gladly boast of my strengths, so that my power rests easily upon me. For Christ's sake, be content with my strengths, my demands, your hardships and calamities. For when I am strong, then you are weak. And you'll need me evermore."

Vignette xcviii

If humans went back in time
Surely the further back they went
They would find the premises
For belief and superstition
Though basic and primal
To be most akin to them,
Since their modern bodies
Resembles nature the most.

For every person there are times; a time to be born, and a time to die; a time to reflect, a time to be responsible; a time to be sick and a time to heal; a time to break down, and a time to build up; a time to weep, a time to laugh, a time to give, and a time to take.

Vignette xcix

The first Existentialist likened anxiety to rubbish
The second to junk
The third to debris
The fourth to trash
The fifth to dross
The sixth to refuse,
And their other perceptions
Also suffers many synonyms.

Consciousness watches over Existentialists. Discourse guides them, delivering them from the disturbing ways of the supernatural and needful belief; which forsake the paths of the simple life and instead walks in madness, rejoicings in confusion and delighting in the perverseness of fantasy; its path crooked and demented.

Vignette C

When winds blow in suburbs
The residents utter
'Here comes the Money-mother
Running over the streets',
And if the winds are hot
There will be recklessness
And if the winds are cold
There will be insecurity.

The beast they fear, that of the loss of a quality life, dwells as though a bottomless pit of despair and is always ready to go on the way of destruction. And those suburban dwellers whose names have not been written in the book of debt will marvel to see the beast, because it is not about them, and it may not necessarily come to them in the future.

Vignette ci

It was the custom

In the old days of superstition

That someone who was sick in the mind

Was called a Crippled Goat,

Limping on one foot

To show the rest

That what was happening on the outside

Was also happening inside.

For though one walks in the flesh, there is no war against it by the flesh. For the weapons of misery are not of the flesh but the mental power which can orientate and disorientate the body. Every objection raised against the knowledge of mental illness makes one captive to it.

Vignette cii

A Chief Executive

Of a highly successful company

Who did not wish it to fall

Passed on his magical powers

To his successor

Who then killed him in the boardroom,

For no business god

Can ever die a peaceful death.

Blessed are those who think of the future, so that they may have the right to climb the tree of success that rises beyond an education. Outside company doors linger the attack dogs and sorcerers and the ruthlessly immoral and cheaters and connivers, and everyone who practices jealousy.

Vignette ciii

A rich man

Who had many wives

Was safe from misfortune

Whilst he satisfied their passions,

And while he did this

His wealth diminished

And then he missed one wife

And a poor son killed him.

The son should have left his revenge to the wrath of his God, for it is written: vengeance is mine, I will repay, for I am the Lord your God and a jealous God. When the son was hungry and thirsty his father should have provided. And God should have heaped burning coals on his father's head, if given the chance.

Vignette civ

The reapers of women
Known as womanisers and ladies-men
Drink their beer in pubs
With other men
Who are home steady,
And to set themselves apart
The reapers call their frothy beverage
Cock-beer.

These womanisers will tarry long over beer, who mix their ego with beer. They should not look at beer when their eyes are red, or when they glare at the bottom of the glass. In the end their beer will bite like a snake and sting like a bee. Their eyes will see strange things, and their hearts will utter perverse things.

Vignette cv

A monarch was so great

That when he farted his subjects did too,

Likewise when he picked his nose

And when he spat on the ground

When he belched

When he sneezed into the air

When he squeezed a pustule

While those who didn't do them were beaten.

If the monarch's subjects ask, it is given to them. Seek, and they will find. Knock and doors will be opened to them. For every subject who asks they will receive, and they who seek will find, and no grief will come to those who do as they are told.

Vignette cvi

In a far-off village, after Summer Solstice
Its biggest entertainer
Takes time off
And is replaced by a temporary entertainer
A fan
Who enjoys the privileges
The Big Entertainer enjoys
Even sleeping with his pet iguana.

And as the time nears the villagers are anxious for relief from this second-class act; and the waiting month is turning from gladness into sorrow and from a festival into mourning; and when they are at the end of their tether, the Big Entertainer returns unannounced, suntanned and fully refreshed.

Vignette cvii

It is the custom of a town

To allow a mock priest

To dispense sacraments

And bless the poor

And pray for prosperity

So that God would favour the town,

And when the real priest returns

He is expected to continue this good work.

And the villagers still ask: 'What good is it if any priest says he has faith but does not have works? Can his faith save us?' A poor person is told by the priest to go in peace, be warmed and be filled. But if faith does not bring with it works, it is dead.

Vignette cviii

Soothsayers observed the weather
To ensure good harvests
And when the weathers failed
The soothsayers paid with their lives,
And over time
There were less and less soothsayers
Until there were none
And meteorologists filled the void.

When it was evening, the soothsayers used to say 'It will be fair weather, for the sky is red.' And in the morning, 'It will be stormy today, for the sky is grey and threatening.' They knew know how to interpret the appearance of the sky, but knew not how to interpret the sign of the times.

Vignette cix

It was believed in an ancient city

That before misfortune could befell it

The protector would sacrifice his eldest son

And doom would be prevented,

But one year a tornado came

And the son was sacrificed

And still tornados came one after another

And the city was totally destroyed.

And in the aftermath the protector slashed his arms and he sprinkled his blood on the city's ruins and all that lay on the ground. Indeed, under the city's law almost everything within it could be sanctified with blood, for without the shedding of blood there is no remembrance of misfortune.

Vignette cx

At the stock exchange
Investors, so as to induce profit
Would mimic the red numbers
Fluctuating on the giant screen
By rising and falling
As if swans in Swan Lake
Prostrate on the floor for long periods
Or dancing in the air.

After a long day and as the investors were nearing their homes, their families and friends would come out from behind high fences in the suburbs to meet them. And they were singing and dancing with tambourines, with songs of joy, accompanied by other musical instruments.

Vignette cxi

A stalk of sweet corn had grown in concrete
In the midst of a crowded city,
And people crowded around it
And they pondered its significance
Wondering why it grew there
When usually corn on the cob is found
Wrapped in plastic
At the supermarket.

And when the city people had gathered together almost trampling one another, the cob spoke, "Nothing is packaged which cannot be exposed, or remain in storage when it can be shelved. What is borne in the ground shall be displayed under fluorescent lights, and what is priced in back rooms shall eventually be proclaimed 'specials' in supermarket aisles."

Vignette cxii

They'd had enough of long drought
In the Outback
And they strung up a bearded man
Who walked in stubbies and thongs
Calling himself Adonis Messiah
Telling anyone who would listen
It will rain if they believed him,
And soon afterwards it did.

For this one spoke in a tongue which talked about the mysteries of the weather and climate. When he prophesied, he spoke to the people for their encouragement and consolation. He couldn't help but boost his standing when he spoke like this. For he who prophesies and speaks in tongues has mastery over others and their insecurities.

Vignette cxiii

To prove that the economy
Causes possession in consumers,
When they stand before a counter
Electronic rhythms are played
While consumers violently tremble
Simulating convulsions
And dancing on the spot in a frenzy
Before they pay up.

Those who buy are of one heart and soul, saying that their purchases are their own, and they have everything in common with the seller. There is not a needy person among them, for they are owners of consumer and household goods and have bought and sold them, the proceeds being laid at the feet of their families.

Vignette cxiv

People with flu are often misinterpreted

When they speak,

For their hoarse and guttural sounds

Sound oracular

Invoking deities of old

Who forebode doom and gloom

When death walks behind

In the cold depths of winter.

People with flu merely pursue relief, and earnestly desire chemical sustenance, since they cannot foresee it. They who offer cures do so for their enlightenment and encouragement and consolation. They build themselves up, for they are greater than those who go about flu ravaged, and they show no signs of it, not even a cold.

Vignette cxv

It has come to be
That humans mimic each other
In the quest for outward perfection,
And some who don't make the grade
Contemplate suicide
In the expectation the afterlife
Will make them whole
And perfect in eternity.

But there are many who are comfortable in their skin, despite the times they lose their self-perceptions to thing which undermine their being causing discomfort. That they are irreverent in behaviour, mischievous and rebellious does not mean they cannot teach what is good, and to inspire others to love themselves, to be self-controlled, and to be kindly to others as to themselves.

Vignette cxvi

When investors seek advice,

Those to whom investors come

Stand on a crate in a prophetic trance

In a shower cubicle

Upon whose heads fall sweet droplets

Of magic waters

Their faces already scarred

By the caress of sharp fingernails.

These financial advisors are expected to be without moral blemish, of good appearance and skilful in all financial wisdom, endowed with knowledge, understanding learning, and competent to stand at the head of the Stock Exchange, and to teach the literature and language of the economists.

Vignette cxvii

Possessed by the spirit of Enlightenment
Filthily clothed men
Shout obscene language
At passing busy people
On the High Street,
For in prosperous times
Complacency and apathy
Are not tolerated by these Holy Ones.

For it is impossible, in the case of these who were once enlightened, who tasted prosperity, who have shared in its knowledge, and have tasted the goodness of bold thinking and the powers of ideas that were and then have fallen away, to restore them again to hope, without them holding frivolous people up to contempt.

Vignette cxviii

Green pears were thought
To be that colour because
The choleric God Misogyny
In his sexual frustrations over women
Would spit at these fruits,
For they resemble
A woman's shape
When they are walking away from him.

What of him, desiring to build a tower of ego, who will not first sit down and count the cost, or whether he has enough gall to complete it? Otherwise, when he has laid a foundation and is unable to finish, all who see it mock him, saying, 'This man can't finish his person because his ego foundation is already too much.'

Vignette cxix

Euthanasia

Is as old as the First Elderly,

And not liking ageing

And having had enough

And fearing decrepitude

He selected a young one

To dispatch him

In the manner of the young one's choosing.

More than that, the youth has learnt from the First Elderly's sufferings, knowing that suffering produces endurance, and endurance produces character, and character produces strength, and strength does not put the old man to shame, because the old man's love has been poured into the youth's heart through his wise spirit now given to him.

Vignette cxx

On colonial Mars
The dead are left to lie where they fall
For it is believed
That good propagation of this barren landscape
Will come of it,
When history tells
That the slain in the 17th century battle of Landen
Had risen from the killing fields as a million poppies.

Martian colonialism is doing it tough, in that its readiness in desiring survival is matched by the desperate need for it. And if the preparations are right, starvation is only acceptable according to what colonists' use, not according to what they do not use.

Vignette cxxi

There was a legend
That a man castrated himself
To faithfully serve the Goddess of Chastity,
And thereafter
Priests of many ancient faiths
Inspired but mortified of the consequences
Wore jockstraps in the shape of the Goddess's hand
Made tight around their genitals.

And behold, a devil's advocate had some of them thrown into prison, that they be tested, and for ten days they were without their jockstraps. They had to be faithful to the Goddess under the pain of death, and only then would they be given back these crowns of life.

Vignette cxxii

There is much blood and gore
At the Festival of Death and Rebirth
Divinely inspired
And celebrated one day of the year;
And the orgy
Spiritualizes priests and worshippers
For the carnage is energetic
And the savagery brutal.

And seeing the crowds, an atheist went up on the mountain, and when he sat down, some friends who had followed came to him. And he said "Blessed are the ragged strugglers, for theirs is the kingdom on this Earth. Blessed are those who mourn, for they shall have comfort. And blessed are the humble, for they shall inherit the future."

Vignette cxxiii

Householders who decorate
The outside of their homes
With Christmas lights
Commemorate dead souls,
Hoping that passed relatives
Will revisit their homes
Guided by the blinking lights
And mournful soliloquies.

For the living know that they will die, but the dead know nothing, and they have no more reward except the living's memory of them. Their love and their triumphs and their failures have now perished, and it is these experiences the living might share with all that is celebrated under a Christmas moon.

Vignette cxxiv

An Australian politician
Made himself a soul-cake
Naming it Ophelia after his dead lover,
Then in a battle for
His party's leadership
He was betrayed
By a woman called Ophelia
Whom he had never met.

He now puts no trust in neighbours; has no confidence in friends; he guards the doors of his mouth from his wife who now lies in another's arms. His son treats him with contempt, his daughter rises up against her mother, the daughter-in-law against her mother-in-law; and his enemies are now the people of his own political party.

Vignette cxxv

To break from the western ideology
Its most powerful women
Inspired by Pelew Island tradition
Have insisted their influence
Be of matrilineal importance,
And great women
Previously unheralded
Shall be western society's inspiration.

Strength and dignity are their clothing, and they laugh at grim times to come. They speak with wisdom, and teach kindness. They look well to the ways of their households and do not eat the bread of idleness. Their children rise up and call them blessed. Their husbands too!

Vignette cxxvi

The God for Tree Planting

And Casual Sex

And known as Sri Pukooh,

Was often represented as a tall fence paling

Wearing a bearded mask

Standing amidst sorghum fields

Draped in a dressing gown

With leafy branches poking out the middle.

And on the evening of the first day of Spring, the doors in ancient villages were locked where families were in fear of the God Sri Pukooh entering; instead waiting until the Virgin God to call. Yet every year, no-one has come to say there is will be peace among them.

Vignette cxxvii

Men were once high priests of beef
And in the worship of beef
They would slaughter a heifer
And roast its flesh over hot coals,
The sacrifices
Held on clear nights
Took place as an epoch
Of hearty carnivorism.

Their beef was always without blemish, this tender heifer. They ate the flesh these nights, roasted on the fire; and with unleavened bread and sweet herbs they ate it. And the flesh was washed down their gullets with beer. And they sang songs of ancient victories. Those were the days when women could not attend.

Vignette cxxviii

So that the human world might not decay

A beautiful and strong god-man

In his natural prime

Was taken to a mountain top

And slain,

Then his blood ran as streams

And was pure and clear

By the time it got to dry lips.

But since human reality is anathema to the expectation of
good things to come, the god-man's blood will never, even
by the same sacrifices which are continually offered every
year, make perfect those who draw down the clear liquid.

Vignette cxxix

'Tis best not to remember

Much of one's youth in old age;

Not by faded photographs

Nor by jumping off milestones

Or by attending

School reunions

When the making of old age

Is the landmark before one's disappearance.

And somehow the years of life may get by reason of strength to eighty. Yet the nearer to the end the worse is the frustration, but thanks to death, the old will fly away. But when the power of anger and wrath diminishes not, still an old one may have time to garner a heart of wisdom.

Vignette cxxx

The last player
To join in rugby drinking songs
Is stripped naked by his mates
Then dressed up in women's attire
And drenched in stagnant water
Then afterwards thrown into a cesspit
And made to walk home,
All in high jest of course.

No greater love has he who has been humiliated by his rugby playing friends. They are his friends because they get him to do what they command. He is more of a player when he calls his mates friends, than when he understands what the coach wants him to do.

Vignette cxxxi

Mountains of remaindered books

Piled into a dump truck

Tipped by the authors

Onto literary agents

Marketing managers

And the assistant editors involved,

Is a sacrifice known

As the Gathering of Dead Books.

Yet not all shall sleep, but some shall be changed to best sellers, at the second printing. And those who love books will work for their good, and also for those who enjoy a good read. And those readers, who foreknow literature and are predestined to not conform to the hype surrounding best sellers, will keep their place at book clubs.

Vignette cxxxii

Before they give their lives
Domestic martyrs are told by priests
They will enjoy the company of gods
In a panorama of domestic bliss
Where the furniture is European design
And where the crockery is disposable,
But they will need the priests
To bless all they've left behind.

Herbs and spices, fine flour, houses, cutlery, fireplaces, refrigerators, packaged food, washing machines, cars, holidays, school uniforms, nappies, relatives, sacrifice, illness, menopause, birth and death; these are some of the spiritual roads upon which domestic martyrs have travelled.

Vignette cxxxiii

From a young age
A child was told
He is the Second Coming
His parents telling him this
Morning to night
While neither he nor they
Questioned the other,
Then the announcement came.

Therefore, stay awake; all of you, for now you know there will be a day when the second child is coming. But also know this. If a master of a house does not know when a thief of the night will be coming, as he fears, he will remain awake every night until the thief arrives.

Vignette cxxxiv

It is not mind filling

To tell a child from an early age

That there is a God

Awaiting the child

At the end of days

Provided its sins are atoned for

Through fear and salvation,

Is it?

Or that prophecy is the sole product of a spirit's will? Indeed, human prophets speak of a God as though they are carried along by knowing its spirit. All God thought is breathed out by God preaching and is made profitable for reproof, for correction, for training in righteousness, and for human prophets to keep up their speaking.

Vignette cxxxv

There was a time

When the Stock Exchange

Was barbarous,

When floor traders

Rushed into the streets

And dismembered strangers

Offering up the body parts

To the gods of Hedging and Options.

If people hated them, know that they hated people first. If the floor traders were known to the community, the community would love them as its own; but because they are not known, therefore the community hates them. And these things floor traders do are on account of their gods, because they forget themselves, and the community do not know of the floor trader's children.

Vignette cxxxvi

In a strange offering to the Moon
Blocks of Swiss cheese
Were assembled by its worshippers
In the shape
Of a human being,
And after the burnt offering
Had finished
They decided not to do it again.

Their hands fashioned it, and now they destroyed it altogether. Then they remembered they made it like clay. Did they not pour out the ingredients like milk and curdled it like cheese? They had clothed it with skin and flesh, and inserted bones and sinews. They had granted it life and steadfast love, but their work did not preserve its spirit.

Vignette cxxxvii

In a famous radio talent show,

A guitar strumming contestant

With one chord and one phrase

Sang 'I love you'

Over and over and over

And over and over and over

Until the judges got the message

Awarding her the top talent prize.

She drew them near to listen better, to demonstrate her mockery of fools, for they did not understand that she was doing mischief. She was not rash with her mouth, nor did she let her heart be hasty to utter any other phase, for love is in heaven and hate is on earth. Therefore, her song's words were few.

Vignette cxxxviii

The success of businesses

Depends on their General Managers

After whose powers diminishes

A payout is then made,

And some employees

Preferred to kill the GM

Before the GM's inspiration declines

Believing their jobs would remain secure.

And those who utter these thoughts are told they deserve a good lecturing, and are given such in the tea room by their middle managers. To employees much has been given, and of them not as much is expected, yet from the GM to whom they entrust everything, they expect the world.

Vignette cxxxix

Cosmetic surgery
For the elderly
Is the best preparation
For the beyond,
It is exclusively for them
To re-enjoy the pleasures
And vanities
Of their youth.

But if the surgeon has botched the surgery and is struck by fate so that the patient dies, there shall be bloodguilt for him. But if the lights went out on him during the surgery and the patient dies, there shall be no bloodguilt for him. Either way he is still going to pay. For eventually his reputation will be acquired by the living families to do as they please.

Vignette cxl

There are some whose personalities
Go astray,
And if they are not liked
No one will seek them
But if they are liked
They are best made like gumboots
Since attractive personalities
Are easily slipped into.

For just as the personality is one and with many variations, and all the variations are of the mind though many, they remain of a single mind, and so it is with the body. If the foot should say, "Because I am not a hand, I only belong to the boot", the hand willingly agrees, for it is a variation of the foot.

Vignette cxli

A girl named Melanie believes

That if she tells all who ask

Who she is

It would mean

Revealing her imperfections,

That is why she has a special friend

Who goes with her

And tells her story instead.

Two are better than one, because each rewards the other for their toil. If one falls, the other lifts up her fellow. But woe to her alone when she falls and her special friend cannot lift her up! When they lie together, they still need warmth, but how will they keep warm? Thus, if new flesh arrives, a threefold cord is harder to break.

Vignette cxlii

There were once powerful wizards
Who looked to punish transgressors
By turning them into insects;
And with traps of bamboo
Made tantalizing and sensual
Wizards would capture them whole
And burn them over fires
Sending the rogue souls farthest away.

But ethical wizards who bolster their weak knees, and make straight paths for their feet, do so to ensure that what is lame may not go out of joint but rather be healed. They'd rather strive for peace with the insects and for their forgiveness, so that there is no root of bitterness in them.

Vignette cxliii

In a high wired asylum out back
A sorcerer psychiatrist with a DSM-IV
Sells mental illnesses to people
Who are displeased with their diagnosis
Either a replacement of their own
Or another not tried,
And the psychiatrist guarantees
They will leave satisfied.

"Fear not," says she, "For I have confirmed you; I have called you by name, you who were once mine. When you go, I will be with you; and praise the irrational, for it shall not overwhelm you; when your diagnosis is a badge you shall not be confused, and the careful shall not criticise you."

Vignette cxliv

When chants of the away team
Are on song after a score
The home team supporters
Wave fluorescent batons in the air
To drive the salacious chants
From out of the stadium,
Lest they descend onto the pitch
And inspire another.

Losers must teach themselves not to be sad, nor to set their hopes on the uncertainty of winning, but on a good game, which richly provides them with everything to enjoy. They are to feel good, to maintain hope, to be ready to praise, so that they may take hold of that which is truly life.

Vignette cxlv

As evening draws in
A building's shadow lengthens
And in it are the ghosts
Of inhabitants' past,
Their genders inconclusive
Their ages irrelevant
Their class unacknowledged
In the egalitarian dark.

The living are surrounded by a great cloud of drifting witnesses. Let the living lay aside every weight, and anxiety which closely clings, and let them run with endurance life's race set before them, and look for bright entrances; for the joy of life is without despising its brevity. Those who bravely peer into them, are able to get on with it satisfied.

Vignette cxlvi

A cleaner who saw and ate
The leftovers from a pop star's banquet
Was told by another
The food he ate was the pop star's own
And he went suddenly mad
And subsequently died,
For the divinity of the pop star
Is as cursed as it is blessed.

The next evening, an Exorcist brought to the cleaner's body people oppressed by demons, and he cast out the spirits with cleansing words and he healed those who were sick. This was to fulfil what was spoken by the prophet Presley: "The dead cleaner took their illnesses and bore their diseases."

Vignette cxlvii

A great Queen would never shake a subject's hand
Without a glove;
Her hand having touched cutlery
After touching her undergarments
After blowing her nose
After wiping her arse
After a bowel movement
Before putting on her glove.

Let them kiss her gloved hand with their sweet lips! For their love is sweeter than wine; their anointing oils fragrant; these virgin men who love her. The Queen brings them into her chamber. There they exult and rejoice in her; they extol their love more than wine; and rightly do they love her, but never would they kiss her arse.

Vignette cxlviii

Should an old taboo remain
That menstruating women are unclean
Likewise women giving birth,
Then it can be said
That seers as well as warriors
The holy as well as the rich
Every male born into this world
Are also cursed with the same taboo.

And on the taboo's eighth day menstruating women shall take two menstrual pads to their male doctor. And the doctor shall use one for a love offering to God and the other for a burnt offering to God. And the doctor shall make his atonement before them because of their natural discharge.

Vignette cxlix

It was a custom in the outer suburbs

For a new hero

To neither chest thump

Nor touch another

Nor walk footpaths threateningly;

In that he remains ordinary

Until an initiated member

Has punched him out.

Older heroes likewise are contained in behaviour, not given to much bravado. They are to teach what is good, and so train the young heroes to respect their peers, to be self-controlled, pure, working in a job, thoughtful, and be respectful to their parents, that their world of outer suburbia may not be so reviled.

Vignette CL

Corporate executives
After a business takeover
Would run office hallways
Shouting and screaming
To drive away the spirits
Of those made redundant,
Lest they
Haunt lunchrooms and toilets.

Some would go across the sea in great ships, doing business on the great waters and hope by chance to see the deeds of the redundant, their wondrous works in the deep end. The Executives mount masts up to the sky; they'd go down to the ocean's depths; their courage melts away in their fearful plight; they'd reel and stagger like drunken sailors who are at their wits' end.

Vignette cli

A murderer on death row
Did a strange thing
And mourned for his victim
By not eating
By not masturbating:
He would starve
Or be executed
Whichever came first.

And at the sounding of the bell the murderer is raised imperishable, and his name shall be changed. For when the perishable puts on the imperishable, and the mortal puts on immortality, then shall come to pass a saying's prophesy, which is written: "Death is swallowed up in remorse." "O judgment, where is your victory? O death, where is your sting?"

Vignette clii

As new legislation went before parliament
The government abstained
From sexual innuendos
And bullying the opposition;
Members rubbed oil on the others' bodies
Slept together head to toe
Confessed their secret desires
And only drank plain water.

That evening, the doors were locked because the government feared the Australian people. Then a kangaroo hopped in, stood among them and said, "Peace be with you." After the kangaroo had said this, it showed them its paws. Then the government were glad when they saw the kangaroo. Then it said to the members, "Receive me Skippy the Bush Kangaroo and the Australian people will be happy."

Vignette cliii

It is enough to know
That danger like belief
Is as real as imagined,
And neither perspective
Can be distinguished
Since the source of a cold wind
Is as troublesome
As the fear of the unknown.

Cold winds blow south and go around the north; around
and around go the winds, and on the earth's circuits the
winds return. All streams run to the sea at high and low
tide; to the place where the streams flow, there they will
flow again. And of the known much will be imagined; and
from the unknown more will be demanded.

Vignette cliv

There was an infallible holy pope
Who had a huge abscess on his lip,
And surely he would have died
Had not a court jester told him a joke
About a man who died on a cross
Whose death cleansed the world's sins
And how he will return to earth
And do it a second time.

This pope's adversary the court jester, this Devil in disguise, prowls around like a roaring lion, seeking to devour him. To resist him, the pope is firm in his sense of humour, knowing that similar suffering is experienced by his brotherhood throughout the Catholic Church.

Vignette clv

To gain victory
Some football teams
Do not refer to their rivals by name,
But rather
As Tree Trunks
Or Jumping Frogs
Or Walking Canes
Or Waddling Ducks in a Row.

For to try and free themselves from loss, they make themselves servants to name-calling, so that their team can win more matches. And they push the sportsmanship of the game that they might win against the strong teams. To the stronger team's fans these name callers appear weak, in that they think they can only win by the use of it.

Vignette clvi

An old man was refused entry to Heaven
And he had all his hair with him
Retained from his long life
For death must leave nothing behind,
And when he asked why
The gate angel said
He had to count them all first
That he be judged correctly.

Further he was told that he shall not pollute Heaven, for dandruff pollutes the atmosphere, and no atonement is made for polluting Heaven unless by the dandruff of the one God who sheds it. And since the old man has defiled his earthly home, he must first dwell in Purgatory for awhile.

Vignette clvii

There was once a game hunter
After killing a bear cub for fun
That his bloodlust was such
He drank the bear's blood
And the bear's spirit entered him;
And he became a bear in the woods
Too frightened to move anywhere
For fear he would be shot.

The fear in him and the dread in him is because of every natural predator on the earth, and of everything which crawls on the ground and every bird in the air. Their fear shall be his fear; their caution shall be his caution.

Vignette clviii

A cunning Haemophiliac
Went around
Spilling his blood on objects here and there
Saying to people they were now his,
Thinking he could exploit a local custom
Whereby an object becomes the Chief's
After spilling his blood upon it.

But soon his enemies collected the blood and threw it into a pit of faeces, and then they threw the false Chief into the pit. Then they said "Behold the blood of the fraudulent Chief who has tried to make us look like fools. See how easily his blood mixes with our excrement!"

Vignette clix

In the top floor of a Great Bank

There dwells a guardian spirit

To be protected

From harm and from injury,

For no hand can touch it

Nothing must cover it

And it sits on the ceiling

So that none may walk upon it.

Some bankers speak in tongues to bolster themselves, for they seek to prophesy and strengthen the bank. They all speak in tongues when they chatter, but their tongues are even more exquisite when prophesying wealth. And the ones whose prophesies are greatest are called in by the spirit to receive large bonuses.

Vignette clx

It is the custom
Among fastidious hairdressers
That as soon as the hair has been cut
The remains are whisked away
For they are a reminder of clients,
Since their hair may either
Beatify those it contacts
Or contaminate them.

The hairdressers judge for themselves. Is it proper for clients to leave the salon with their heads uncovered? And does not custom teach that if a man has long hair it is a disgrace for him, but if a woman has long hair, it is her glory? For long hair is given to glorify a woman's sensual skin.

Vignette clxi

A young girl disliked her brother so much
That she stole his bodily refuse
His clipped nails, snot and faeces
And wrapped them in gum leaves
Burying them as an effigy in the backyard
Casting a spell upon it
So that when it decayed
So then would her brother.

And thus, she began her career practicing divination and fortune telling. She became a sorceress, a charmer, a medium, a necromancer. She inquired of the dead, wore magic bands upon her wrists, and she made veils for the heads of persons of every status. She also hunted for troubled souls in her suburban neighbourhood.

Vignette clxii

In certain ancient customs
It is taboo to transfer blood
From one body to another
Or from body to earth,
Unless as kindred spirits
Each nurtures the other
And bears immaculate fruit
For love of the community.

As an apple tree is among trees of an orchard, so are public servants beloved to each other. With great delight they give each a taste of their ink, and the fruit of it is sweet to their tongue. They go together to a night bath-house, and they declare their mutual love. Sustained with passion, refreshed with beer, they are sick with bureaucratic love.

Vignette clxiii

In order that the mail be delivered

Village people unlock everything

Undo everything tied

And leave nothing crossed,

In this way the mailman

Will come unimpeded out of the mountains

That lay beyond the horizon

Bearing the News of the World.

The mailman often makes a way through the sea, a path in the mighty waters, and brings forth chariot and horse, army and warrior; together they go forth, they rise on high, they are distinguished, star like and quick. He also makes a bold way over uneven footpaths, and bridges over turbulent waters.

Vignette clxiv

A jealous lover
Made sure that his rival
Will not possess his love object
By having his rival's
Penis tied in a knot
And his scrotum squeezed
When he gets too close,
As if by magic!

And if this rival's hands cause further sins, they will be cut off and thrown away. And if this rival's eyes cause further sins, they will be torn out and thrown away. And it is better for the jealous lover to have his rival live a lame and blind life rather than throw him dead into a bog of quicksand, to be then forever yearned for.

Vignette clxv

If an ancient rapscallion had spun
Seven times clockwise
And seven times clockwise
And did not pull out dizzy,
There was a chance
That none of
The Seven Deadly Sins
Would have shown up to this day.

He was once a Spirit, who sat on a throne in Heaven. And he had the appearance of jasper and carnelian, and around the throne was a rainbow which had the appearance of an emerald. From the throne came flashes of lightning, and rumblings and peals of thunder, and before the throne were burning seven torches of fire.

Vignette clxvi

So that visiting supporters
Could protect themselves
From the home team's evil spirits,
Each would pour beer onto scarves
And wrap them around another's neck
To be worn during the match
Demonstrating the bonds between them
And intoxicating them besides.

Some visiting supporters have woes. Some have sorrow. Some have strife. Some are complaining. Some have mental wounds without a definable cause. They can tarry long over beer; they can get drunk on home brews. In the end beer bites like a shark and stings like a wasp. Drinker's eyes see strange things, and their minds imagine perverse things.

Vignette clxvii

A woman facing redundancy

Sought the help of a sorceress,

Who prepared sweet foods and drink

To be offered at the guillotine

Operated by a man under pressure

Praying he is not the one

To release the levers

When business gets really rough.

This is the same woman who walks blamelessly and does what is right and speaks truth in her heart; she who does not connive nor does evil to her co-workers, nor does she take up reproach against her superiors; she who swears by her own hurt, who has worked hard all her life.

Vignette clxviii

So that husbands return with their pay,

Wives so as to praise them

Refer to their husbands

As Eagles in the Sky

Saying to their children

Our Eagle is coming home soon

And when it lands

We will have money to live by.

At home wives empower tired husbands who must accept their responsibilities, for as new fathers they are weary like their wives, and they are exhausted. And yet fathers who are patient with their wives shall renew their strength; and they shall fly again with wings like eagles; and they shall work and not be weary; for they work for their wives who shall feel appreciated.

Vignette clxix

A tribe in the outer suburbs
Were given new cars
On a day when huge hailstones rained down,
And they trashed them all
Because novelty and disaster
Do not sit well together
In the minds of a people
Too used to struggle and strife.

The tribe speak as though they are people who have not
loved, that they are like noisy gongs or clanging cymbals.
And if they have war-like desires and understand violence
and its methods, and if they have the desire to take things
not theirs and do not care, they are like rolling and
tumbling boulders.

Vignette clxx

There are some cultures now
Which don't mention Economics,
And when they talk money
They say Keynes vs. Hayek
Or Government intervention
Or the freefalling Free Market
Because the word Economics
Has taboos attached to it.

They who feed the wind will not sow, and they who follow clouds will not reap. And if they do not know the way money comes to wallets and bank accounts, they do not know the work of Economics. In the morning accounts should be checked and at evening fear should be withheld, especially by those who doubt their prosperity.

Vignette clxxi

The supernatural past is dead,
And no matter how much revival
Is attempted by theologians
And other custodians of that past
The fact remains that nothing
Of how it was can be spoken of
And be given a true account
Other than it is 'the lost one'.

How lucky for theologians that this past has not been seen,
from the beginning of the world, nor will it ever be. For if
those days had been cut short, the truth would be
remembered. And fortunately for the reputation of
theologians those days cannot be cut short.

Vignette clxxii

As is the custom in Hollywood

When a child of an actor is born

A designated director would choose

The role of a past actor

And give it to the child

So it can live like that actor,

And many have been known as

Jimmy and Dorothy.

Whoever of these child actors does not follow the least of the rules of acting and encourages others to do the same will be called last when there are new roles, but whoever of them follows the rules and shares them will be called great in the world of entertainment.

Vignette clxxiii

Upon the circumcision

The father threw his son's foreskin

Into a freezing salty lake

In the hope

That his son's future promiscuity

Will bring contraception,

And no pox

To scar a conquering past.

And a conscious dishonouring of their bodies they heed, and they exchange their old selves for the truth about who they are as men, long guilty of self deceit disabling their being. At home over a glass of wine they talk of women from whom they have taken natural relations for conquest and pleasure. Then they return to the lake and together they fish for the son's foreskin.

Vignette clxxiv

His feet never touch the ground
His hair and nails are rarely cut
The sun is unworthy of warming him
His eating implements
Are for him alone,
He is friendless and retired
And too great
To be admired.

And when his presidential term ends, this dear leader will step away from all the power and the legislation and enter literature, writing abstract stories about himself and mocking democracy. Directorships and veneration are soon to come and no ordinary person will challenge him because he will never walk his country's streets.

Vignette clxxv

Misfortunes which befall people

Are put down to

Fetishes and curses

Associated with the sea,

And none must dwell on it

Nor swear on it

And to fish from it

Is to draw up hatred.

A being had created an expanse in the midst of the waters, so that the expanse separated the waters from the waters. When the being made the expanse, it separated the waters under the expanse from the waters above the expanse. And it called this expanse luck. Then the being let the waters under luck be gathered together into one place, but unfortunately chance then appeared.

Vignette clxxvi

A false minister of religion
Is akin to The Holy Wrestler,
One righteous
Whose lips will touch no other
And who wears a shiny garment
Sleeping rough
And is the first to wrestle Demons
For their threats are many.

The role of the Holy Wrestler is untrustworthy because his tasks are unrealistic. They are actions which threaten wisdom and are akin to adding a dead rat to perfume. The smell advertises the Holy Wrestler when he walks the footpaths; for to everyone passing he is a fool.

Vignette clxxvii

Homicidal men

Who suffers fits of rage

Manic and then peaceful

Are revered by Fanatics

As ones who are their shadow,

For when Fanatics decide to kill

They in their violence

Add more to tragedy already blighted.

Fanatics need not be anxious over who should be killed or what mayhem they will make; nor need they drip-feed God into their alienation. Is not life more than these things? Look at the birds in the air: they neither pray nor kneel nor gather in religious halls, and yet people love them. Fanatics are nowhere near as vital to life as birds.

Vignette clxxviii

The soul departing the corpse
Replicates the body
In fragrance and outline
Leaving the body
Weightless and wispy
To gather with infinite lifelessness;
This is Death
In the language of Imagery.

"I'll tell you a mystery," said the poet. "We shall all sleep long, and we shall all be changed, in a moment, in the twinkling of an eye, at the last hurrah. For the hurrah will sound, when the dead are perished on the earth. The buried perishable body must put on decay, and the memory of the person must put on immortality."

Vignette clxxix

A General Manager of Finance
Had attained the position
At lunchtime in the canteen
On January the First one year
As a pretender to the position
In a cock fight with others,
Witnessed by the unambitious workers
Until one thereafter stood.

As an aside, the staff are to be submissive to their new boss in everything; they are to be well-pleasing, not argumentative, not pilfering, but showing every good faith, so that they may adorn in everything the directives of the General Manager, and therefore renounce rorting, skiving, back stabbing and malingering.

Vignette clxxx

For the particularly famous
Words to describe their behaviour
Are created only for them;
Words for when they eat and sleep
Fornicate and defecate
These unique words
Which separate them
From the fandom of their world.

Not many fans will become like the famous, for they who enter fame are judged with greater scrutiny. And if a becoming famous person stumbles over indiscretions, he or she is reduced to mere ordinariness, unable to bridle a whole career. How great is failure set ablaze by a great gossiping fire!

Vignette clxxxi

Male Movie Stars believe

They are the reincarnate of Kamadeva

Making believe to women

That by carnally knowing them

They can enjoy true bliss

With divinity;

And the women make believe to Kamadeva

That their passions are truly sacred.

A eunuch asked, "Whom shall I bring to you?" And Kamadeva said, "Bring me Aphrodite." When the eunuch saw Aphrodite, he let cry a loud whine and said to Aphrodite, "Why have you deceived me? You can't be Aphrodite. Instead, I see an old woman standing in earth." And Aphrodite said to him, "What is appearance? I lust like an old tigress."

Vignette clxxxii

When mothers

Have had enough of pooey nappies

And other domestic disquietudes

They are said to have a holy spirit

Invade them to comfort them;

And their husbands adore them

As they are no longer a wife

But a Queen to them.

Domestically mothers cannot be subject to their husbands, even when they hear their words, for they have their husband's respect when they see their wives in this way. The mothers' adorning is in their strengthened heart, and they are possessed with the glowing beauty of a patient and determined spirit.

Vignette clxxxiii

Only by force shall dissent be suppressed
The force of time and history
The force of repeated words
The force of weaponry;
Some dissent is gouged from rock
Carved and made art
And placed upon a pedestal
A likeness to something.

There are things tyrants hate, and which are an abomination to them. Bright eyes and questioning tongues. Minds which shed orthodoxy, and hearts which devise common sense plans. Feet which hastily run from big brother and lungs breathing clear air; and also, those who reap words from dissent, making them honourable and fresh.

Vignette clxxxiv

The King of Rain
With the belly of a Zeppelin
Carries heavy storms
Which erupt each spring
When gifted by farmers
Who threaten to rip open his belly
If it doesn't rain,
Or if the King dislikes their gifts.

Once there was nonstop rain and it brought a great flood. Only one farmer and his family and flock survived. By fortunate coincidence the farmer was a bathtub collector. And soon he fashioned a vessel for his brood to sit in and to float upon the rising waters. Eventually they met the King of Rain and they gave Him new gifts.

Vignette clxxxv

Only Sacred Kings

Do not die a natural death

Thinking of Jesus and Kennedy

And Caesar as another;

For their reputations

Would be lowered

If their extraordinary lives

Ended ordinarily.

But get this. From their presence even soils and bacteria flee away, into space and beyond. The sea looks for the dead who are in it, Hades give up its dead that fries in it, and Death itself seeks to go by a different name. If these Sacred King's names are not written into history, all who love them are left bereft and empty.

Vignette clxxxvi

Olympic swimmers
Famous for their gold medals won
Famous for their endurance,
Had their severed birth cords
Cast upon raging seas
In the belief
They would become
Great competitors.

It is well known that in a swimming race, only one receives the major prize. None swim aimlessly; they do not kick as one kicking the air. They discipline their bodies and keep them under control, lest after swimming hard they should be disqualified. Thus, it is generally accepted that it is not only self-discipline which sustains them.

Vignette clxxxvii

Little is left of God belief

When one's eyes and ears

The senses which feed one's brief being

Go with the fruits of living

Landscape and the weather

Friends and all that uplifts one

And it is enough,

More than enough.

Thus, two friends are better than one and then both should be well rewarded for their toil. For if one falls, the other will lift the friend up. Again, if two lovers lie together, they keep warm, better than one who tries to stay warm alone. And the loner will prevail against being shunned when self-esteem is stronger than self-pity.

Vignette clxxxviii

As a tribute to the Financial Analyst
A co-worker
Danced naked upon the Analyst's desk
To the charivari of rock and roll music;
Crouching
Then jumping like a monkey
Demonstrating the Analyst's
Physical strength and mental agility.

The Analyst then seizes the dancer, poking two fingers into the eyes, and binds the dancer with handcuffs. The head is shaved and the dancer is left in a dark room until the hair grows back. The dancer is lead back to a clean desk, for by now, the Analyst has re-discovered where the money grows and has written a management report about it.

Vignette clxxxix

The extracted submission

Induced by fear

Has meant the person

Feeling it

Had their will submit

To the disease of fundamentalism,

For toxic air

Favours the oppressor.

Whosoever resists will incur more fundamentalism. And be afraid of those who exercise it. They think they do what is right, for they are servants to righteousness. And if infidels do wrong, be afraid, for fundamentalists say they have every right to be avengers who carry out their wrath on wrongdoers. The weak must be in subjection, not only to avoid their wrath but also for the sake of conformity.

Vignette cxc

Her heart passed through the hands

Of her mother

And her mother's mother

And her mother's mother's mother

And it was not tainted

By disappointment

When returned to her,

And thus she is ready for love.

Hers is love patient and kind; unwilling to envy or boast; nor will she be possessive or rude. She will not insist on her own way; she will try not to be irritable or resentful; she hopes to learn from her wrongdoings, and rejoice when finding out the truth. And accept too, that there are things which will go beyond disappointment.

Vignette cxci

To kill infidels is meaningful
For Allah's warriors
Who will leave the world as martyrs
Having fought to the death;
And on fulfilling the Prophet's wish
They die with erections
Ready to meet
Heavenly virgins above.

Some martyrs, when they meet the painted virgins, hate them because they doubt their virginity. Then Allah comes to show them the evidence of virginity. Allah will proclaim "Here is the evidence of their virginity." And Allah spreads the virgins under garments before the martyrs for them to see. And these martyrs argue with Allah. And furious, Allah sends them to Hell still erect, and to Eternal Celibacy.

Vignette cxcii

If there must be a soul
Place it as words
On a tombstone,
Words which describe
The person's life
As though it were not in vain
And written with empathy
For the living.

Therefore, since death is surrounded by so great a cloud of
witnesses, let death also lay aside every weight, and also
despair which clings so closely, and let death run with
endurance the race that is set before the living, who, for the
joy of life set before them, may endure their sufferings with
dignity.

Vignette cxciii

As the soldier walked over a landmine

His young soul was burned

As was his uniform

Manufactured back in his homeland

That was a totem

To strike fear in the enemy

Who remain unknown,

To others and to themselves.

A poet travelled from Paris to Baghdad to sing this soldier's praises, and he fell among fanatics in the desert, who beat him to near death. A struggling entertainer, passing by saw him, and remembered compassion. He went to him and bound up his wounds, and then he took the poet to a hotel to recuperate leaving him there, but not his words.

Vignette cxciv

And they stripped the politician naked
And clothed him
In tracksuit pants and t-shirt
And for awhile
He pretended he was ordinary
And one of the people,
Before a sorcerer had revived him
And he felt dead no more.

The sorcerer's name was Byron. He practiced magic in the city and amazed the people with his tricks, saying that he was somebody great. His audience paid attention to him, from the poorest to the richest, saying, "He has the mental power of Alexander whom is called the Great." And they were enthralled by him because he says he does it for the greater good.

Vignette cxcv

Around the totem of the Dollar

Dance men and women

Singing investor songs,

For abundance

Does not come without cunning

Nor without the inadequacy

Of the poor

Who cannot dance as investors can.

Come now say the poor. You the rich may weep and howl over any discomforts which come upon you. Your riches could rot and your garments may be moth-eaten. Your ornaments might corrode, and their corrosion will traumatise you and it will eat your wealth like fire. And while you lay up treasures in expected down days our discomforts are our daily life.

Vignette cxcvi

When the green effigy says Go

Pedestrians should walk straight

And not amble

Lest the course

Of their lives

Arrests,

And the future of their dreams

Baulks and turns back.

Wisdom shouts aloud in cafes, in the shops she raises her voice; at the head of noisy streets she cries out; at the entrance of the Town Hall she speaks: "How long, O easy ones, will you love being easy? How long will gamblers delight in their gambling and will the ignorant scorn knowledge? Behold, I will pour out my spirit to you; I will make my words known: but come seek me first. "

Vignette cxcvii

Should the native bird
In the hunter's sights
Clasp together its claws
In mid flight,
The hunter might turn away
Cross his arms
And cross his legs
And cross his gun with providence.

The hunter shall dwell with the deer, and the poacher shall lie down with the young elephant, and the fisher and the lion and the fattened sow walk together; and a little child shall lead them. The nursing child shall play over the crushed guns of the hunter, and the weaned child shall put a hand in the poacher's hand and in the fisher's hand.

Vignette cxcviii

For warring armies to succeed
In the deserts of the Middle East
Their leaders must be motionless
In their fortresses,
For if they move
The turbulence from their arguments
Will rise
And their grunts will be destroyed.

Now it is that war has arisen anew in Minds; Conscience and its agents fight against Belligerence. And Belligerence fought back hard, defeating Conscience, and there was no longer any place for it in Minds. And Conscience was thrown down to the sands, and its agents were thrown down as well. Common Sense followed, as did Empathy, and Anxiety now spreads far and over the sands.

Vignette cxcix

As is a custom of Capitalism,

The needy on a given festival day

Discard their rags

In favour of wealthy attire

To then go around the streets

Mocking and abusing whomever they meet

And giving vent

To their natural frustrations.

And they shout aloud, not holding back. They lift their voices like trumpets; declare to the world the transgressions of the wealthy, and of the Stock Exchange and its contrivances. And yet some well-dressed needy quietly seek the wealthy out to tell them how they are beacons of goodness, in the hope they might secretly set up charities in their names.

Vignette CC

He loves God

Said the madman

To his psychologist;

Thus prove God said she

And the madman said no

And he was let go

For who is to say

That in delusion there is no belief.

The madman set up a tent calling it a Holy Place. In it stands a lamp and on a blanket are the remaining crusts of his physical presence. There stands an urn covered on all sides with blue plastic, and within, a clear cup holding his mind, and the scripts of his treatment. Above it hover the cherubim of sanity. His chair he calls the Mercy Seat.

Vignette cci

There was once a priest

Known for beating his penis

With a cucumber,

When asked why

He unzipped his fly

Showing the questioner

The enemy

That lay within.

He would repay one guilty moment with another, never giving a thought to doing what was honourable before the concern of his Church. It was not possible, so far as he needed help, for him to live peaceably with himself at all. He was always avenging himself, the wrath of sex; for he would say, "Vengeance is mine, I will repay myself."

Vignette ccii

There was a time
When the mother
Kept her mouth shut
During childbirth,
An impossible task
One might say
But her energies were needed
For the Discussing Jungle.

And it is there she negotiates her fate. For if she bears a male child then she shall be unclean for seven days. As is during her menstruation, shall she be unclean. And on the eighth day the male is circumcised. If she bears a female child, then she shall be unclean for two weeks as is her menstruation, and then continue her purifying for a further month.

Vignette cciii

Breasts drawn on a boy asleep

Is no mischief,

For when this boy wakes

His feminine dream fulfils

The boy's wish

That he will now be

Quite different

To what he was born as.

For his thoughts are his illustrator's thoughts, for his ways are the others' ways, declaring now he to herself. For as the heavens are higher than the earth, so are his illustrator's ways higher than his ways, as indeed are the motives. And one day his mother will reveal herself as the one who drew, for she had always wanted a beautiful daughter.

Vignette cciv

At night
On busy city streets,
Those who randomly
Punch down strangers
Are vicious enough to scapegoat
Their troubles
And cowardly enough
To boast.

And as for those of them who love it, their victims will send cursing misery into their hearts, in their homes and where they work. The sound of their cracking skulls shall put them to flight, and they shall flee as one flees from violence and strife, and they shall fall even when there are no pursuers.

Vignette ccv

In a conversation between

Two women

Esteem flew from out the mouth of one;

And the other upon seeing her distress

Found it

And upon returning it to her

Saw that her growing sickness

Was no more.

The gatherer was a doer of her word, and not a speaker only. For if she was simply a speaker of her word and not a doer, she is then like someone who looks intently at their natural face in a mirror and then goes away and quickly forgets what a face is really like.

Vignette ccvi

Behind mirrors lurks Unlikeness

That if given a chance

Will drag the looker

Through the mirror,

And the horror

Of the person's lost Likeness

Is then far too much

Even for the wretched Void.

If anyone worships their Unlikeness and receives a red mark on their forehead or on their hand, they will drink the wine of Likeness's wrath, poured full strength into the cup of its anger, and they will be tormented with fire and sulphur in the presence of their parents and also in the presence of Mickey Mouse.

Vignette ccvii

Beware smiling politicians

Bearing great promises

In exchange for your vote,

For after they get it

Few policies will get traction

And instead

Like a portrait photographer

They have taken your soul.

They had visions: plans for welfare and not for self serving, to give the people a future and hope. They were approachable at election time, like that of a shopkeeper, a customer, an office holder. They would listen to problems and to ideas for a better future. They would discuss the future for the children to grow into. They even planned to work for their community.

Vignette ccviii

Should dogs die out
Humans will give the species
A new name if they return
For none will speak of them in their old name
In reverence to them,
Because the lives of dogs
Fill people with great joy
Because of their loyalty.

A God will be dreamt up who'll say "Blessed are you, the dogs, for your kingdom is mine. Blessed are you who are homeless, for you shall be nourished with food and with love. Blessed are you when people are cruel to you and eat you and use your name "dog", when they are insulting."

Vignette ccix

Nobody was asked

Why he is Nobody

And not Napoleon or Buddha

Or Somebody at least;

And Nobody replies every time

That if he had another name

He would only utter it

In an indulgent and offensive manner.

Nobody does nothing from rivalry cr conceit; and in humility counts others more significant than himself. Nobody looks to the interests of others. He has this mind within himself, who, though he is in the form of God, counts equality with knowledge to be grasped, making himself nothing, taking the form of an idea, being born in that likeness.

Vignette ccx

A belief was held
Long before there were public toilets
That to satisfy the urge to go
Pilgrims risked losing their souls
When they emptied their bowels
Roadside in front of others;
So they'd hang on until journey's end
And release on the nearest chamber pot.

Also, they feared losing the secrets of the Kingdom of Heaven. Yet to those who were good and lose, more would be given, and they will have abundance, but those who were bad and lose, more will be taken away. But those with constipation could not know whether they were good or bad.

Vignette ccxi

At a restaurant famous for gastroenteritis
The master chef and his staff
Eat what is prepared
And sit with the patrons
Discussing the five-star menu
Creating a bond
Between customers and staff,
But not every night.

Inasmuch as the staff has undertaken to compile a narrative of the things which have been accomplished among them, just as those, who from the beginning were eyewitnesses to when the master chef's fame has been delivered, it seemed a good idea to them also, having kept an eye on the different menus, to write an orderly account of the gastroenteritis outbreaks.

Vignette ccxii

Only the Sun is ruler
Over the seas and lands of Earth
Over all nations
Over creatures' great and small;
The air and miasma its rays strike
The void within its sweep
The shapes which alternate
Between darkness and light.

When the Sun falls it has all night to get back to the place from where it rises. A vulnerable time when destruction comes like a murderer, and the skies pass away with a roar, and the galactic bodies are burned up and dissolved, and the Earth and its works are exposed.

Vignette ccxiii

There was born a child

Who grew

To knows the habits of the President

Where the President lives

How many advisers the President has

What the current foreign policy is

What the unemployment figures are,

And when she will be President.

And behold, presidents reign in righteousness, and lawyers
rule in justice. The eyes of those who see stay open, and the
ears of listeners give attention. The hearts of quibblers
understand and know, and the tongues of procrastinators
speak warily. The opposition are noble, the corrupt are
called to account.

Vignette ccxiv

A mutual worshipping society

Was formed

By an Exclusive sect

Each believing the other to be the Christian god;

Exclusively mingling between themselves

Jesus among Jesus'

Trinities among trinities

Gods the Fathers the Sons and the Holy Ghosts.

In fits of righteousness, they'd seize secular books, these modern Tempters, and bind them in dark vellum, and throw them into a deep hole, and they'd shut it and seal it over so that the books might not deceive God's ears any longer, until a thousand years had ended. After that the books might be released to be read; just for a little while.

Vignette ccxv

In a remote corner of the globe
The shepherd is revered as a deity
And none may touch the shepherd
Except another;
When all must worship the shepherd
As the shepherd worships the Sun
Since together they are
The life givers.

This story is trustworthy. If anyone aspires to the office of shepherd, they desire a noble task. A shepherd must be above reproach, the friend of sheep, sober-minded, self-controlled, respectable, hospitable, be able to teach, not be a drunkard, not violent but gentle, not quarrelsome, not a lover of money. Then the flock will be managed well.

Vignette ccxvi

A woman in white
Believed she was integral
To the Godhead
And had sinful men follow her;
And after their divine communion
The men shed their inhibitions
And walked
Naked in the world.

She persuades the men to take millstones and grind flour, to take hoes and till ground, to seek out the poor, and walk beside them on streets and highways. Their skins are uncovered, and their sins seen. They work in silence, and they go around in humility. They were the sons of Beelzebub, who is no longer the master of their once crooked destinies.

Vignette ccvii

A new Messiah

Cannot be recognised

For he will speak in all languages

And live in suburban opulence

Pronouncing doom

Upon those who do not conform

And then he'll withdraw his friendship,

This Saviour of Mankind.

There remains much messiah confusion while the new Messiah renders judgment to each human accordingly: and to those who by patience in well-doing seek for affirmation and piety and satisfaction, he will give a good reference; but for those who are self-seeking, who do not obey the rules for trust, but obey unrighteousness, there will be the usual wrath and fury.

Vignette ccxviii

How to wound reckless people
Who are an enemy,
Is by finding their shoe prints on pathways
Tyre marks on highways
And impregnate them
With curses
So that they will be lame
And their vehicles impounded.

But do not fall in love with them. You hate them but you might want to do them good. You might allow them to hit you and you won't hit back. They might want to take things from you and you might give them more! And you might wish what your enemies do to you, but you would not wish them do it to themselves!

Vignette ccxix

Through gardens she walks

And a man who loves her from afar

Gathers after her footprints the soils

And places them in a terracotta pot

And in the pot there grows

A single white rose

Its petals then withering,

As will his love too distant for her.

No emotion has yet overwhelmed the strength of this man. He is faithful, and he will not let himself be tempted beyond his capacity to thwart it. And through his romance he will find a way to encounter her that he may be able then to endure it. But before then, he will grow another white rose.

Vignette ccxx

The ancient worship of trees

Replaced by the modern use of trees

Replaced by the preservation of trees

Replaced by the mass felling of trees

Replaced by the modern worship of trees;

And then there was one

Drooping and withering

Panicking the people into unconditionally loving it.

Revived it became the tree of life with twelve kinds of fruit, ten of grains, seven of fish, and thirty-five different kinds of vegetables. The leaves of the tree heal the sick. Its branches bear the dwellings of several nations. In its trunk are buried the dead. And its roots feed on blood and bone.

Vignette ccxxi

It has been for generations
A belief passed on
To young sponge-minds
Impressionable and happy
That there is a god,
And if sceptical minds are wary
It is because
Truth can also grow from bad seeds.

To sponge-minds are given stories, and they are told in their abundance. As it is, in not looking at what they see, and in not listening to what they hear, they absorb uncritically. Indeed, it is prophesied that young minds hear but never understand, and see but never perceive. Then it is the task of repetition to contrive credible answers when young minds expand into questions.

Vignette ccxxii

Remarkably for Great Forests

They are not merely atoms and molecules

Water and bark;

They are inhabited by supernatural beings

Which come from rains and winds and fires

Above

And from clays and soils and silts

Below.

When anyone comes into the lands and mountains of trees, they shall learn to follow the inhabitant's practices. These are practitioners of water divining, drought telling and weather interpreting. These are beings who inquire of the health of the dead, and others which care for animals. And there are others who hunt for tree fellers and arsonists.

Vignette ccxxiii

It is a custom still
For couples to make love
Beneath a billowing tree;
For if they make love
On the East side
They will bring into the world a boy
And on the West side
To the world a girl.

The children always thank their parents for forming their inside parts; knitted together in the mother's womb. They know they are treasures wonderfully made. Their identity is secret when made in the hidden, intricately woven in the depths of wholesome mother-flesh. Their unformed substance is slowly given direction; for which they also thank the tree.

Vignette ccxxiv

When it was believed
Animals had spirits
They were apologized to
When they were hunted and killed,
But no apologies
Have ensued
Since it is believed
They do not.

For at one time hunters were in the light of need, but now they are in darkness. They walk as children of darkness, for the fruit of darkness is found in all that is covetous and unnecessary, and they discern only what is pleasing to them. Animal lovers take no part in these unfruitful works of darkness, but instead expose them.

Vignette ccxxv

A Catholic priest,

Possessed by Satan

Recited his child molesting ways backwards

Blessed his bishop's silence

Crossed his chest with gold and silver

And canonised a corrupt pope

At midday

In an empty cathedral.

A crowd had come to watch but stood outside, and a man named Jesus Christ went in and said to the priest "O faithless and twisted generation, how long am I to suffer this appalling church? How long must I allow it to bear my name?" And Jesus rebuked the Church, and Satan came out of the priest and he was healed.

Vignette ccxxvi

Speculators who made prophetic failures

Are set around in a circle

Where lays a bleeding corpse;

And at a given signal

The faulty speculators rush at the body

And engorge on the corpse's entrails

Before they sit satiated at their desks

To prophesy the money flow once again.

But it is better speculators speak in a language for the every-person and not in tongues for themselves; for no one understands them. They merely surround the movement of money with mystery. The ones who speak of the money-flow in ordinary tongues need no interpreters, nor do they need academics to support them.

Vignette ccxxvii

The Oracle of Lung Cancer
Each year is heard to scream
And enter into violent spasms
When it inhales
The smoke of a million cigarettes
Placing the Oracle in a trance,
For it to then predict the outcome
Of every smoker's inhalations.

The Oracle knows that coughers will leave their last day with coughing, and defending their smoking desires. They will say, "Where is the promise of giving up? For ever since the tobacco leaf there have been cigarettes, it's been the same as it ever was." And yet they deliberately overlook the fact that lungs existed before cigarettes.

Postscript

Francis Bede now invites the reader to journey through a grey portal in Alfonso's long years of bright living, for through there is found shadows of despair which marred his young heart. Across the bridge of time, is a melancholic scene which a romantic poet could only depict as tragic; when the troubles of love and loss fiercely prevailed, exacerbated by the cunning machinations of a gangrenous faith. Imagine yonder, a dim bedroom of an inner-city terrace, embowered amid Jacaranda trees and a flowered and scented garden, close by the gurgling waters of a neighbour's voluminous fountain, a scene in which gentle afternoon breezes will never more fan Alfonso's beloved Marion's apple blossom cheeks; she, his first wife, who is now tragically dead, and he laying prostrate on their marriage bed, in deep mourning.

The moonlight of an August evening is gilding the rich Victoria Gardens nearby; the native foliages have not quite lost their radiance, and birds are foraging in the undergrowth. The Gardens, which so lately resounded with laughter ringing like church bells, the music of a merry heart, are deadly quiet. The drawn curtains of Alfonso's home hide the heart-struck and the dead. On a wall is the exquisite picture of a young Marion, gazing onto a regal bed on which Alfonso's foetal figure lays shrouded in his gloom. It is thought that pictures of dearly loved ones have a clairvoyant power to possess those who loved them in life. If this is so, then on that August night the dead Marion saw clearly into the despairing Alfonso in their conjugal bed. His broad manly brow, over which his brown hair unfurls in graceful curls, is buried in her pillow. His full lips are locked in a kiss, and his closed eyes and recumbent form, are seeking her presence.

Previously, in the year 1924, at the age of twenty-three years, Alfonso was given at the altar Marion, the daughter of Mr and Mrs Smythe. When they walked from the ceremonial podium to the outside as a married couple, delicate flowers were strewn in front of the wedded pair over which they merely glided, leaving the flowers undamaged. Such was their love for each other. And for just over one married year their life was a scene of bliss.

Alfonso and Marion wore the latest fashions when they went dancing the Charleston at jazz venues. They were just as fashionably dressed when they went to the movies. Their home, nearby to Alfonso's adoptive parents, was a modest yet ornate two-story terraced house. Their circles of friends were society wide. And then tragically, in the next instant, Alfonso was standing by the side of his dying wife in hospital, struck down in childbirth; his beloved Marion yielding her last sighs. He buried her by a silvery gum in her church graveyard. The lily blended with the white rose, and the gum overshadowed the grave. It was here where Alfonso the widower came to rest in the evenings. He lost all interest in Jazz, the movies, and he felt no need for company.

In his depression Alfonso would go into his backyard and gaze at the evening skies, and unsettled thoughts bedevilled his mourning mind. When he saw the sun sink to the west, adorning the clouds with its glorious rays, he mused on religion, looking for answers as to why he should suffer such grief. He fancied he saw a Heaven and a God, and traced in the lines of even-light heathen worshippers of the animus and spirits. He looked at the Sun and its worshippers, those who sought the origins of purity there, in the origin of all that is good on the Earth. He looked at the fables of Greece, and found delight in the lyrics of Sappho which told of love and beauty; at Egypt, where the priests, in their esoteric rituals, searched for the sources of life, and motion, and joy; and then, in his deepest gloom, he imagined the Christian heaven, but here all was dark and slimy, like the caverns of Dante's Hell. He wished to meet his Marion again, not in Pagan life rituals, not in Christian parables, but in the world of realities.

To lift his depression, he felt the only answer was in the world around him, in society, at work, in writing, and in family. Only there, in the day-to-day affairs of life which fully occupy industrious minds, would he find happiness.

And most of all he wished for a new wife to be mother of his boy-child, the affectionately named Charlton; a mother like his sainted dead. There was but one who answered his ideal; alike in features, in passion, and in grace to the lost Marion. Born of the same parents, loved by Alfonso as

239

though he was her brother, similarly educated and imbued with in-common thoughts, Florence was the image of her dead sister, his dead wife.

With deliberate and compulsive emotion, the love of Alfonso for Florence soon passed the bounds of that of a brother-in-law; longing to make her his wife, he adored her with the passion lavished on the dead Marion. The intense gaze of his deceased and beloved Marion encouraged him to bestow all his affection on the younger Florence. She had cared for their child with the pride of an aunt, and she saw her sister's eyes in the laughter of the happy babe, saddening her, her grief close to the surface of her emotions. She also loved Alfonso as a man. For, though he was not blessed by the god of handsomeness, he did however, possess a bounteous personality.

Florence was doing the duty she felt she owed to her sister Marion. But Alfonso sought to unite with her, she who was in Marion's likeness, so intuitive were his sensibilities towards her. They often would communicate without exchanging a word. Alfonso had not felt this with any other female companion. Over time Florence became anxious to marry Alfonso; her love for him intensifying. But there existed something which, to her mind, was greater than human duties, and it frustrated him. God and her Church demanded her first attention, and then her lover and his child, but not before Alfonso acquiesced to the Church's rules. The Church, in cruel mockery of her love, worked to confuse her affections for Alfonso with her love of God. The Church condemned Florence's choice to live in the married home of the infidel Alfonso, as though they were lovers, until he converted to the correct faith of Catholicism. She wanted to pledge her love to Alfonso at the altar, but her priest had mocked Alfonso's affections for her.

This attitude enraged Alfonso and the opportunity to rebuke the Church was too good to be lost. He had married his beloved Marion in the church to please her, but his scepticism overtook him, and now it was time for him to act. Florence felt the force of Alfonso's arguments when she wandered with him through the nearby Victoria Gardens. While he talked, her confusion was too great even to notice the scented flowers. A heart sick for love, a mind wandering from her sister's grave to her child, made her potentially a widowed maid, for she knew she could never love another man. To overcome her scruples, Alfonso would write a tract, inviting the clergy to refute it, defending his marriage with a deceased wife's sister. But ere as he spoke there came the same dark scene within Florence's mind.

At night in her anxious imagination there stood a gaunt priest, with black canonical robes before the gates of Heaven. Behind him and through him was the way to eternal happiness, below him was the fiery Hell; and he shouted with a hoarse voice at her, 'your love is incest!' And as he shouted, he pointed with his scornful finger at her and then at this Christian Hell, and she conjured up in her mind the cruel face of this priest, and she saw livid flames rising up higher until they encircled her body, and meanwhile the priest screamed with fury "incest is anathema, an anathema to God and to your Church!' And in terror she lay on her bed, with the big drops of sweat dripping from her brow, her heart rapidly beating, her mind wildly distracted.

Her Catholic creed, its dogma, its sermons, and the doubts it sows when it's perceptions of sin perverts its judgments of others, have caused Florence great discomfort. And yet it is uncanny that she and Alfonso are so comfortable with each other. And her features, she has been told somewhat resemble him. For she too has not been so blessed by the goddess of beauty. No, the Church was jealous of her. And not only that, the Church confuses a devotional love between two young people with that of a priest's devotional love for the Virgin Mary.

Florence Smythe was miserable; for she was placed between her love of Alfonso and her duty to him and her religion. Had she been a woman of stronger will, she would have torn her Catholic creed into shreds; she would have dared the Church's prejudice, the ostracism of its accusations; and clung onto the man she wanted so truly, in defiance of something she could easily have dismissed with the power of her natural love.

The arguments in Drill's tract were conclusive (the above discourses demonstrate them), but she was still too young

243

to trust reason. The obviousness of common logic is of the Devil's making. Florence Smythe, true to Alfonso, loved him; but true to her religion, she dare not marry him without the approval of the Church. So Alfonso as a last resolve, laid the matter bare before the Archbishop of Melbourne at a meeting which included a bishop and monsignors, and from these ecclesiastical leeches, behind their canonical arguments, there was a shrill prejudiced cry of infidel, infidel! And those terrible insinuations came mockingly to the ears of Alfonso, making his home like a bedlam-house; he ranting and raving like a souped-up lunatic, which nearly sent his loving Florence to an early grave. Still, she stood by him.

Denied the status of wife, she still acted as mother to her sister's babe, the boy known affectionately as Charlton. There was a calm heroism here. But the passionate Alfonso could not handle further insults. The last kick of bigotry against this broken-hearted Freethinker was given. Into a funk he again sank. He could no longer rise with the magpie, and roam his floriated back yard garden. To him the birds, as they warbled, spoke of joys never to return. The Yarra River told him of recent days when he and

Florence floated on its waters in an elegant row boat; and even his jazz loving friends only too bitterly reminded him of the tournaments of wit they jousted in the presence of his engaging deceased wife. His life was scene one of misery. He saw no chance of amendment. In a fit of mad despair, he tied a rope around his neck and hanged himself.

But this was a thwarted suicide, for Florence found him too soon for the angel of death to claim him, and cut the rope and revived him. And for hours he lay in her arms in the same state of despair as he had after Marion died. Not a word was said of this attempt thereafter; Alfonso's memory of it muted by oblique denials and the hope for future happier days.

The scene of the pale form of Alfonso's, with dishevelled hair and weeping eyes, in grief, who lay over the rapid upheaving swells of Florence's fair bosom tells of her affection strengthened, not just by love, but also by compassion. Alfonso nervously grasped Florence's hand, then how he rises and implants kisses on her lips! His hair, which yesterday was glossy as the crow's, is now as bleached as fresh snow; to-day he utters plaintive cries, to-morrow he'll dream of joining his new wife in their bedroom.

Ideally, in loving families which are replete with caring members, none should need end their life; and at worst for an individual if there are no dependents, nor friends, it is the needs of society, through its medical professions, which must give succour. But, at the same time, the sole purpose for one's existence is for happiness. If Alfonso cannot find happiness in life, if he's believed that life has conspired against him, he could be justified in taking up arms against it; and thinking that suicide is the best weapon, he felt free to nurture the impulse with that focussed thought. And yet, in defiance, if he bore up against his overwhelming feelings of hopelessness, rather than madly attempting to eradicate them, he would have saved himself through courage rather than being saved through luck. Florence saw Alfonso at his lowest, at his most vulnerable, when his raw vulnerability could be wounded by even the cockiest jab of the lowest Catholic priest. And not long after Alfonso's recovery Florence married him in a civil ceremony.

www.ingramcontent.com/pod-product-compliance
Lightning Source LLC
Chambersburg PA
CBHW020403120726
47904CB00002B/691